SOPHIE BRIGGS AND THE RAGING SERPENT

SOPHIE BRIGGS AND THE RAGING SERPENT

THE SCHOOL OF ROOTS AND VINES™ BOOK EIGHT

MARTHA CARR
MICHAEL ANDERLE

DISRUPTIVE IMAGINATION

DON'T MISS OUR NEW RELEASES

Join the LMBPN email list to be notified of new releases and special promotions (which happen often) by following this link:

http://lmbpn.com/email/

This book is a work of fiction. All of the characters, organizations, and events portrayed in this novel are either products of the author's imagination or are used fictitiously. Sometimes both.

Copyright © 2023 LMBPN Publishing
Cover by Fantasy Book Design
Cover copyright © LMBPN Publishing
A Michael Anderle Production

LMBPN Publishing supports the right to free expression and the value of copyright. The purpose of copyright is to encourage writers and artists to produce the creative works that enrich our culture.

The distribution of this book without permission is a theft of the author's intellectual property. If you would like permission to use material from the book (other than for review purposes), please contact support@lmbpn.com. Thank you for your support of the author's rights.

LMBPN Publishing
PMB 196, 2540 South Maryland Pkwy
Las Vegas, NV 89109

Version 1.00, June 2023
ebook ISBN: 979-8-88541-858-4
Print ISBN: 979-8-88878-441-9

THE SOPHIE BRIGGS AND THE RAGING SERPENT TEAM

Thanks to our JIT Readers

Diane L. Smith
Jeff Goode
Dorothy Lloyd
Christopher Gilliard

Editor

SkyFyre Editing Team

CHAPTER ONE

"I sure am gonna miss this old place."

Walter Briggs stood with his arm around his daughter Sophie's shoulders over Spring Break. He was staring at Thicket Hall and had tears in his eyes.

"I know, Dad." Sophie studied the graying bark of the behemoth tree that doubled as the main building for the School of Roots and Vines. It had been infested with two death spikes the previous week, spikes made by Gregory Templeton and stolen by Caleb Justice and Connor as they raced each other to open the last seal keeping the Serpent in the Realm of Chaos. She hadn't felt comfortable leaving her old friend, so her family had opted to come to campus.

She was the life Defender, after all, and it was her job, along with the other Defenders, to make sure Thicket Hall stayed alive as long as possible. They had to prepare for the battle to come and be ready after the lovable tree succumbed to the death magic in the spikes.

Sophie patted her pocket and felt for the familiar lump of the acorn the tree guardian had given her, a glowing golden seed that contained Thicket Hall's psionic presence and all its memories. It would be her task to replant the guardian after the battle, provided she and the other Defenders survived it.

Miss all of you, I will, Thicket Hall told Sophie. Its voice was louder and clearer than ever before, with it being so close to her now. *I will always be here, but like to be full of warmth and food and saplings, I do. Not want to be a sapling myself.* An intense loving protectiveness washed over Sophie, and she chuckled.

Don't worry, old friend. We'll take good care of you, and maybe in a few hundred years, you can be a school building again.

"Where will all the classrooms and offices go?" Millie, Sophie's thirteen-year-old sister, asked. "It won't look the same when I come in September, will it?"

"Probably not, Mills." Sophie ruffled her hair. "Thicket Hall wants you to know it'll always be here, at least in spirit." She drew the acorn out of her pocket and let Millie hold it.

Millie grinned as its golden glow lit up in her palms, responding to her life magic. She closed her eyes and took a deep breath. "I can't hear it like you can, but it feels friendly and very, very old. Like the redwoods we saw in California."

"Exactly, sis." Sophie draped an arm over her sister's shoulder. "You're gonna be a tree girl just like me."

"What else would she be?" Joyce, their mother, put in with a laugh.

"Hey, Briggs fam."

Sophie turned to see her fellow Defender and death

elemental fiancé Marcus Jenkins and his dad Robert heading their way. Marcus tossed his long, platinum-blond hair out of his eyes and waved.

"Hey, son." Walter pulled Marcus into a hug, then Joyce did the same.

"Hey, big brother!" Millie tackled Marcus in a hug, and Marcus laughed and squeezed her tight.

"Hey, little princess." Marcus ruffled her hair, then turned to Sophie and kissed her cheek. "How's Thicket Hall?"

"Millie's visiting at the moment." Sophie chuckled, nodding at her sister's hands. She was examining the acorn again, turning it over while Walter, Joyce, and Robert looked over her shoulder.

Marcus sighed. "I hate that this place won't be the same when she comes here."

"Yeah, I do, too." Sophie watched her sister's radiant face as she explained to the adults what she felt from the acorn. "I think she'll be okay, though. So will everyone else who comes here after this is said and done because if we do it right, there won't be any more threats from the Serpent. She can just exist and learn and be a normal kid like we didn't get to be."

Marcus nodded, and his eyes flashed with a mix of nostalgia and bitterness. "Yeah. I think it'll actually be better when you put it that way."

Sophie leaned her head against his shoulder. "Definitely."

After a dinner of Ned's Chicken and lots of warm hugs from family, Sophie and Marcus made their way to the pond under the light of a near-full moon. When they got close to the water, they heard quiet voices. Moonlight glinted off the lenses of two pairs of glasses, and Sophie smiled. It seemed they weren't the only couple who'd come here.

"Hey, Simon," she greeted. "Hey, Janet."

"Oh, hey!" Janet Humphries, an earth elemental and Sophie's long-time roommate and fellow Defender, giggled and waved. "We can leave if you want."

"No worries, sis." Marcus plopped down on the empty bench and patted the seat next to him for Sophie. "We can all just hang."

"Now all we need are Liv and Cedric, and we'll be a Defender party of six," Simon Green quipped. He was another of Sophie's long-time friends and their water Defender.

"I think they're at Sonic," Janet noted. "They can't stop eating mozzarella sticks."

"I heard that." Olivia Wright, the fire Defender and Sophie's long-running frenemy, stepped into the clearing and glared playfully at Janet.

Janet laughed nervously. "You can eat all the mozzarella sticks you want, Liv."

"Uh-huh. I'm sure it helps that I brought you guys some?" Olivia gently shook a brown paper bag covered in grease stains.

"Oh, man. Those are delicious." Simon eyed the bag, practically drooling.

"Don't worry. There are enough to go around." Cedric

Justice stepped up behind Olivia, carrying an armload of paper bags. He was their air Defender and was the most recent addition to their team. His blue eyes flashed with amusement as he noticed Marcus and Sophie on the bench. "Of course, I didn't know we'd be feeding the entire Defender lineup. I would have brought more."

"How much are you planning on eating, man?" Simon protested.

Cedric tossed him a bag and laughed. "Oh, that's right. You've never seen me eat." He handed a bag to Sophie, and the six gathered around the bench to dig in.

"These are amazing," Janet gushed after a few moments of contented chewing.

"Tell me about it," Marcus agreed.

"Figured we'd all earned it after…you know." Cedric's eyes took on a new darkness. No one elaborated on his words, but everyone knew the loss Cedric had faced when Gregory Templeton killed his uncle to save Sophie's and Marcus' lives.

"For sure," Sophie agreed gently. She glanced at the sky as she ate. The moon had washed out all but the brightest spring stars. She picked out Leo the lion above them, and deep toward the east, Arcturus glinted like a red-orange beacon, like an omen of what was to come.

"Nothing is the same anymore," Janet noted after a heavy silence. "We'll be graduates in a month, and everything feels like it's coming apart at the seams. Even the ground feels less stable, like it knows what's coming." She glanced down at the ground as she spoke.

"I know what you mean," Simon added. He wrapped his

arm around her shoulders. "The pond has been more restless lately."

"Same with the air," Cedric agreed. He bit into a mozzarella stick and glanced at Liv. "Hope you haven't been playing with fire too much."

"Yeah, I don't need another charred backpack if things go haywire with our powers again," Janet joked.

"In all seriousness, I think a burned backpack is the least of our worries this time." Marcus sighed. "If we can't get our ducks in a row by the time Thicket Hall leaves us, we'll be at a serious disadvantage. The whole world is counting on us, magical and non." He gazed at them all. "We've got to find a way to pull through when it counts."

Sophie touched his shoulder. "Beyond strategies and maneuvers, though, we have to stick together. When all else has failed in the past, we've always been able to rely on each other."

Marcus nodded, and the determined edge in his eyes softened.

Sophie looked at the others. "Things are really crazy, and it's good to make sure we have a plan and that everyone's on board with it. If we can't keep our Defender bond strong and give hope to the others, we won't stand a chance."

Olivia grinned. "That's why *you're* here, Miracle Grow."

"She's right," Janet added with a smile. "You always find a way to rekindle hope and bring out the best in everyone. We need that now more than ever." She looped one arm around Simon's shoulders and the other around Olivia's.

Olivia rolled her eyes, but she did the same to Janet and Cedric.

Sophie giggled. She sat on the ground and pulled Marcus down with her, and soon all six Defenders were in a loose group hug.

"Aren't we the cutest?" Sophie gushed.

"If by cutest you mean the mushiest and covered in fast food grease, then sure," Olivia snarked. "We fit the bill."

Sophie laughed and repeated her mantra, the phrase that allowed her to transform into her pure elemental form.

"Defenders are better together," she declared. A shockwave of golden energy raced through her and ricocheted around the circle. Everyone's eyes lit up yellow-orange in the dark, and everyone had a smile after the glow of the magic faded.

"Hope is going to win this battle," Janet declared softly.

Everyone murmured their agreement. Marcus kissed Sophie's cheek.

"Don't ever change, princess," he murmured. "We need your light."

Sophie nodded and leaned against his shoulder. She would do her best to keep her friends full of hope, light, and life, and she had to believe that would be enough to face their greatest and craftiest enemy yet.

CHAPTER TWO

April continued on in the aftermath of the battle, and by the time classes restarted on the Monday following Spring Break, the campus looked relatively normal. Thicket Hall still towered above the grounds, and it remained sturdy enough to continue to be used as a building. Many of the professors made changes to their final exam requirements as students and faculty alike lined up outside of Headmistress Rogers' door to ask what they could contribute to the welfare of their beloved school. Sophie's final grade for Advanced Life Fundamentals rested on her efforts to sustain the tree's waning life energy.

"If saving the school for the thousandth time doesn't count as one heck of a final project, I don't know what does," Garver had told Sophie as she clapped her shoulder. "Besides, can't have you wearing yourself out too fast. We still have roses to dye for graduation!"

Sophie, though grateful, had groaned as Garver chuckled teasingly.

After lunch, Sophie headed to Roscoe's workshop to grab another jar of his neon-green ointment for Thicket Hall's graying bark. As she approached the familiar wooden door, a cacophony of meows broke out, along with faint scratches.

"All right, you little ingrates! Scram! Outta my way."

Sophie chuckled as Roscoe opened the door, his hair disheveled and his eyes bloodshot.

"Oh, it's you," he rasped. "Got any banana bread?"

Sophie handed him the loaf tucked under her arm, which he took with hungry eyes.

"Don't be so mean to the kittens, Roscoe," Sophie playfully scolded as she stepped inside. "They're just happy to see me." She crouched to rub the persistent kittens' ears. "Where's Princess?"

"Under the table," Roscoe replied. He stirred a pungent concoction on the stove, then dumped it into a jar for Sophie. "Been a little skittish since what happened to her baby."

Sophie nodded soberly, then studied Roscoe's frantic movements, his furtive eyes darting around as if he were looking for trouble and his shoulders rigid.

"How are you doing?" she asked quietly.

"Me? Oh, I'm dandy," Roscoe snarked. "Once again, we find ourselves trying to save Thicket Hall from not just one, but two death spikes at the hands of your beanpole's doppelgänger dad, of all people." He flipped madly through a recipe book, added a dash of something to the hot liquid he'd just poured into the jar, then closed the lid.

"On top of that, I find out it's not going to matter in the

long run beyond buying us some time." He slammed the book shut and heaved a frustrated sigh. "How many things does a man have to lose before he's done? I had to bury my buddy. I lost another cat a few months ago, and now—" His lip trembled, and he cleared his throat forcefully. "I'm losing my life's work. To think I'd be alive to see the day that eight hundred-year-old giant fell." He wiped his eyes.

Sophie's heart ached. She stood, peeled back the foil on the banana bread, and silently cut Roscoe a slice.

"You won't lose Thicket Hall," Sophie reminded him gently. "It'll look different, but you'll still have work to do, trust me." She patted the acorn in her pocket, and Thicket Hall's warm presence rushed over her. Turning to Roscoe, she handed him the slice of banana bread, then pulled the acorn from her pocket.

"New beginnings are hard," Sophie began. She tucked the acorn into Roscoe's palm.

He stared at it in confusion.

"It's the acorn Thicket Hall gave me at the end of the battle," Sophie explained. "It'll regrow from this seed. Sure, we may not see it fully grown in our lifetimes, but its presence will always be here, and it'll always be a guardian for the school, the students, the staff, and the channels, like always. From death will come new life, Roscoe, and you'll be here to welcome it and take care of it." She smiled encouragingly at him.

Roscoe's eyes sparkled as he stared at the glowing gold acorn. He touched it gingerly, then pressed it to his chest.

"That helps," he croaked. He smiled at Sophie and pulled her into a rare side hug. "Thanks."

She laughed and patted his broad shoulder. "Of course."

"Sorry I couldn't make this a whole date, my queen." Cedric peeked at Olivia, who was halfway through her order of mozzarella sticks in the Sonic parking lot. "Gotta head back. They want me to work with Sophie on the leaves."

"It's fine," Olivia soothed. She patted her mouth with a napkin, then touched his arm. "I mean, I'd rather us keep doing this than deal with the you-know-what."

Cedric shuddered. "That's for sure." He bit into his burger and absentmindedly stared out the window. Olivia noted his bloodshot eyes, and her heart fell.

"Hey. I know things are rough right now, but how are you dealing?"

"Not well," Cedric admitted past a mouthful of food. "I've always been a junk food guy, but it's all I eat lately. Can't keep gains at the gym. Don't feel like going most days."

Olivia nodded. "You know that's not healthy, Ced."

"I know. With how busy we are, though, I don't know what else I'm supposed to do. Going home to cook dinner or trying to make it the night before never works. Besides, since Uncle Caleb…" His voice trailed off, and he stared angrily at the burger in his hands. "Well. Anyway."

Olivia frowned. He'd been avoiding the subject of his uncle's death for the last week, so she had been unable to help him. She knew it would take time and patience, but supporting him through it? She had no idea how to do that. If he would cry on her shoulder like he had the day it happened, if he would walk through memories with her

—*something* to ease his grieving heart—she'd feel useful, even hopeful.

As it was, he'd withdrawn from her in many ways. Maybe he didn't feel comfortable enough with her. Maybe the wound was too raw. She was trying to respect his boundaries, but where did boundaries end and unhealthy withdrawal begin?

Olivia grasped his chilly hand and squeezed it. His emotions were a whirlwind of grief, shock, and a desperate need to drown the pain.

She let her hand warm with enough fire magic to be comforting.

Cedric put his head on her shoulder. "Thanks, queen. You're always here for me, even when you don't say anything. You don't know how much that's helped."

Olivia pressed her cheek against his head. "I've been worried about you."

"I know. I can see it in your magic. It's just too much to talk about right now. It feels way too big, like it'll swallow me whole if I even try to approach it." His voice broke. "It's terrifying."

Olivia gave his hand a reassuring squeeze. "I know."

"I'm also scared of messing up or becoming like him," Cedric went on. "I'm a Defender now. I've inherited his legacy, and it's not a good one. I mean, I loved him so much." He sniffed, and a tear dropped on her sleeve. "I loved him, but that doesn't mean he was a good person or even a sane person. I don't know how to make sense of it. I don't know how to carry on when my heart can't figure out this puzzle."

Olivia stroked his honey-blond hair, reassuring him she was listening and he could talk as long as he needed to.

"I've been part of this family mafia for almost a decade. I helped him hurt people. I didn't understand what I was doing, and I trusted him and loved him with everything in me. I still love him, Liv. It doesn't make any sense." He shook with sobs, and Olivia held him as tears pricked her eyes.

"Love doesn't always discriminate between good and bad. It just exists," Olivia whispered. "It doesn't make you wrong for loving him."

"I wanted him to get help," he choked. "I didn't want him to die."

"I know."

"Why the hell did he have to hate the Templetons so much?" Cedric's voice rose in anger. "Why couldn't he let it go? He'd still be here, dammit!"

Olivia shifted and let him fall against her chest as his angry outburst gave way to heart-wrenching sobs. She held him tight as tears streamed down her cheeks. If there was one thing she'd learned about the grief process, it was like setting a bone over and over, never getting the placement quite right. It felt okay for a while after the dam of emotions burst and the storm swept past. Then it built again, as strong as ever.

They were only a week in, and Thicket Hall was counting on them. How was Cedric supposed to bear this crushing weight?

"I don't know," Cedric responded to her unspoken thought, his familiar, prickling presence brushing her mind. "All I know is I can't do it without you."

Olivia smiled reassuringly. "I'm not going anywhere, my king, and for the record, you're doing an amazing job. I know it doesn't look or feel like it, but you're doing the work. You're showing up. You're here for all of us. We all see it, and we appreciate it more than you know."

Cedric didn't respond, but the brighter colors swirling in his magic made Olivia smile.

CHAPTER THREE

Marcus sat at the desk in his office on the Friday morning after Spring Break. A phone number waited for him to dial it, scribbled on a sticky note attached to his monitor, but his hand hesitated over the old-fashioned number pad of his office phone.

He took a deep breath and punched the numbers in before he could rethink it, then pressed the receiver to his ear and drummed his fingers on the desktop.

"High-Security Warden Roberts speaking," came the answer after a couple of rings.

"Agent Marcus Jenkins at the EBI," Marcus responded with all the authority he could muster. "Put me through to the Templetons."

There was a pause. "What kind of clearance you got, Jenkins?"

"Lead agent on the Thicket Hall case," Marcus replied with a strategic hint of irritation. "Working directly with EA Interim President Trevor Bruckner. Put me through, please."

Another pause. "Five minutes. That's all I can get you."

"That's plenty." Marcus gulped as the warden transferred his call.

The line was picked up after two rings. "Who is this?" demanded a shrill voice. Darla. Marcus sighed. If he told her who he was, she'd never give the phone to Gregory.

"I need to talk to your husband." Marcus lowered his voice, hoping she wouldn't recognize him. "I'm from the EBI."

"Listen, if this is about what happened to Justice, you have to understand, darling," Darla ranted. "He was only protecting his son."

"Let me speak to him," Marcus insisted.

"He has the right to remain silent!" Darla protested.

"Darla!" Marcus snapped. There was a stunned silence, and he massaged his temples. Great. Not even 9 AM, and he'd yelled at his mother. "Listen. It's Marcus. I need to talk to Gregory, please. I've only got five—"

"Marcus!" Darla gushed. "Why didn't you say so, darling?" Her voice softened as she spoke to Gregory. "Darling, darling, our son called! Can you believe it?"

Marcus facepalmed. "Darla, please. I only have five minutes. I need to ask him something."

"Well, of course, darling. Here you are. Goodness me, why didn't you just say so from the beginning?"

Marcus suppressed the urge to heave a sigh. There was a shuffling sound, and then Gregory's silken voice answered.

"Marcus?" There was an edge of disbelief in the word.

"Yeah, it's me," Marcus replied. "Listen, I have to ask you something." A tone sounded in his ear—one minute had passed. "We need your help. Thicket Hall is fading fast, even with everyone helping. We're not ready to face this thing yet. You got any other ideas?"

Gregory sighed. "I was afraid of this."

Marcus waited for him to elaborate, and another tone sounded—two minutes gone.

"I don't have much time," Marcus warned him.

"The only advice I have for you at this point is to use what little time remains to gather your army. Recruit as many willing souls as you can find, and recruit agents from EBI agencies across the Eastern Seaboard."

"Okay." Marcus nodded and scribbled on a sticky note.

"Feathering is also still missing, correct?" Gregory asked.

"Yeah," Marcus grumbled. Yet another piece of the puzzle they didn't have any control over.

"So, you are planning a war on two fronts," Gregory explained. "You don't know the time or date of either enemy's arrival, and you only know the battleground for one of them—the school. Get as many components of this battle under your control as you can. Hunt Connor if you have the agents to spare. Continue to slow Thicket Hall's death until your reinforcements are in place. You need as much control on your side as possible."

"Understood." Marcus nodded, his heart sinking with dread. Another tone, this one repeated, urgent—one minute left.

Marcus gulped. He'd called for advice, it was true, but he also needed to know something.

"Um. Do you have a date for the trial yet?"

A pause. "Not yet."

"Are you able to call out, or can you only receive calls?"

"I can call out once a week," Gregory replied. His voice was hushed, almost expectant.

"I'm giving you my number," Marcus declared before he could change his mind. "Let me know as soon as you have a trial date."

He dictated his number to Gregory, who had Darla write it down on a napkin.

"May I ask why?" Gregory murmured.

Marcus chewed his lip. He didn't have an answer for that. He didn't know if his torn heart would ever make sense when it came to the Templetons.

"I—" He began, but the line went dead.

"Your time has expired," announced a recorded voice. "Goodbye."

Marcus sat with the dial tone in his ear for a good minute, then hung up and sighed.

Gregory's words had done nothing to soothe the dread in his heart. In fact, they'd had the opposite effect. He'd nearly forgotten about Connor in the rush to try to preserve Thicket Hall, which was likely the way Connor wanted it.

He'd always been crafty, but using Simon's Defender power against them in the last battle meant that no matter how strong they were, Connor would be just as strong. He was an elemental chameleon, and, like the Serpent, he loved to turn their greatest strengths against them to gain the upper hand. They'd have to be vigilant if they hoped to keep him at bay.

Come to think of it, he ought to do something to make sure the Defenders weren't Connor's target. It was entirely likely that he'd try to hurt one of them before the Serpent made her appearance.

He picked up the phone again and hit a few buttons. "Hey, Trev."

"What's up, bud?" Trevor greeted him.

"Think we ought to have escorts for the underage Defenders around campus?"

There was a pause. "What's got you worried?"

"No one has seen Connor since the fight. If he's her host, it'd be in his best interests to make sure there's as little resistance as possible when she comes back."

"Ah. Got you." Trevor sighed. "Well, I'm sure you'd do the honors for your fiancée, and Cedric would kill anyone who tried to touch Miss Wright, so that leaves two."

"You and Dot want the job for Simon and Janet?" Marcus quipped. "It'd get you out of the office."

"I would, but I'm pretty swamped. I'll get Trish and Desiree on it. They're two of our best."

Marcus nodded. Olivia's mother and the secretary they'd rescued from Colorado would make the perfect guardians.

"Good idea, bud. We can't be too careful with that trickster on the loose."

"While we're at it, do we have any spare agents who could try to find him? The less we have to worry about when this thing emerges, the better."

"Wish I could say we did, but most boots are on the ground at the school," Trevor replied.

"What about regional offices? Can we get some transfers?"

"I'll see what I can do." Trevor paused. "I take it you talked to your old man."

Marcus' heart flipped. "If by 'old man' you mean Templeton, then yes. He advised we keep a strict watch out for Connor."

"I see." Trevor sighed. "Any news on the court date?"

Marcus hesitated. He didn't like the alarms ringing in his intuition, screaming that Trevor could sense the change happening in his heart.

"No," he muttered.

"Hey." Trevor's voice took on a fatherly quality. "You know I ain't here to judge you. Your heart is big enough to encompass people who might not deserve it. You're not wrong to forgive, even if some of us aren't as generous as you. You understand?"

"Got it." Marcus shifted uncomfortably in his seat, then cleared his throat. "Gonna head back to the school now. Got a fiancée to protect."

Trevor chuckled. "See you later, bud." The line went dead, and Marcus headed out, his head spinning.

CHAPTER FOUR

Sophie saw a lot more of Marcus as April ran out of days. He'd been assigned as her personal guard, so he escorted her to every class.

"You always were a gentleman," Sophie teased as they headed toward Thicket Hall for their morning rendezvous with the other Defenders. "Now that you don't have classes anymore, you can walk me all over campus."

"Got that right, princess." He walked with his hands in his official EBI jacket pockets, glancing around the campus with alert eyes.

"It's gonna be an exhausting day," Sophie continued. "We're helping Thicket Hall, and then I have to go dye the last truckload of roses for Garver."

"She's making you dye your own graduation flowers, huh?"

"Yep. Charlotte and I do it the quickest, so she has us picking up everybody's slack," Sophie snarked.

"I meant to tell you," Marcus began. He leaned closer and dropped his voice. "I picked up my tux yesterday."

Sophie beamed. "Really? How's it look?"

"Looks good." Marcus shrugged. "I mean, my outfit is *not* the main event; let's be real. Besides, if Nate has his way with the garment bag, I'll be dressed in ribbons. Had to stuff it in the back of the closet."

Sophie chuckled. "Oh, Nate. He would. I will go pick up my dress this weekend with Mom, Charlotte, and Mills. Gonna make sure it fits one last time. You know, in case I ballooned up in the last few weeks." She rolled her eyes.

"Nobody's gonna be gaining much weight until after this ordeal is done, I don't think," Marcus remarked. "Too much energy needed to keep our old friend kicking, and too much stress waiting for the inevitable."

"Yeah." Sophie's smile faded. "Did you find out anything from Gregory Templeton?"

Marcus shook his head, and his eyes turned stormy. "He reiterated what we knew, and he reminded me about Connor. Yet another thing we have to keep track of that I nearly forgot about."

"Well, that's still helpful," Sophie countered. "Now the Defenders are protected, too. That's worth a lot."

"I guess so." They were nearing Thicket Hall, and Janet, Simon, Olivia, and Cedric waved them down.

"Time to get to work." Sophie sighed, patted Thicket Hall's acorn in her pocket, and rolled up her sleeves.

A couple of hours later, Sophie stepped into Thicket Hall on wobbly legs, followed by the other Defenders. They'd given their all to break yet another massive death magic "clot," as they call them so Roscoe's neon-green concoction could nourish the damaged tree.

"So. Hungry." Janet clung to Simon as she walked.

"At least we made some progress." Olivia sighed and mopped her sweaty hair out of her eyes. Cedric blew a gust of air over her face to cool her skin.

"Good work today, guys," Marcus agreed. His skin was paler than usual. "Let's get some chow so we can think straight."

They piled their plates high with sandwiches, chips, salad, and pre-packaged snack cakes. Even the cafeteria staff was strapped for time. Everyone was working around the clock to keep Thicket Hall strong and stable, so there were fewer hot meals nowadays.

After everyone had eaten, Sophie took the acorn out of her pocket and gently set it in the middle of the table. Thicket Hall reached out and touched all of their minds, warming them with affection and winning a tired smile from everyone.

Hey, you old grump, Marcus greeted. *How are you feeling after our work today?*

Much better, Thicket Hall replied. *Roscoe's medicine good. Keep my roots healthy, most of the way. Some death sickness still gets past into my boughs. Expected that. Good work, you did. Bought much time.*

Everyone's shoulders slumped in relief.

You still don't think we'll be able to save you? Janet's heartbroken question made Sophie's heart ache.

Not in long run, sapling, Thicket Hall replied sadly. *Wish you could, but feel it in my roots and bark. Like Roscoe's cat. Like kitten you try to save.* The tree's rumbling presence filled Sophie with comfort even as her heart fell. *Still, everything helps. Is not in vain, saplings. Will make time, delay chaos until you are ready.*

What if we're never ready? Simon put in. He glanced at the others. *We're just kids. Strong, yeah, but kids all the same.*

Unstoppable, you are. Watched you defeat enemy after enemy over past three years. Have done more for me in short time than most have done in entire life, you have. Defenders not chosen by accident, sapling. Something special, the six of you have. Big hearts. Big power. Always doing next right thing. Learning from mistakes. Loving and trusting each other.

As the ancient tree spoke, Sophie met the eyes of the other Defenders, who returned her gaze with tenderness and trust.

Much expected of you, but great will be your reward, Thicket Hall concluded. *Known forever in history as Defenders. Celebrated as heroes, you will be. Knowing you protect what you love, always. No one will take from you.*

What about the past Defenders? Cedric asked. His blue eyes shone with moisture. *They didn't do their job. They were corrupted. We don't even know who all of them were.*

Thicket Hall's hum vacillated thoughtfully.

Is true that Defenders are not chosen by accident, it replied slowly, as if it were considering every word carefully. *Old generation is renewed by the younger. Qualities long buried under greed and obsession rise to surface—love, protecting what is worthwhile, friendship, trust. Even if did not win out in the end for one of them.* The guardian's words dropped to a gentle whisper on the last phrase as Cedric's eyes welled with tears.

I understand. Cedric nudged Olivia's shoulder, and she hugged him.

As for the other, Thicket Hall continued, speaking to Marcus this time, *true it is he may lose his life when all is said and done. Similar to my death, will not be in vain. Saved you both, protecting what he loved at the cost of one he used to love. Could feel it in his magic. Big heart, he also has. Just like you, sapling. Did not want to do it. Had no choice.*

Marcus set his jaw and nodded, refusing to look at the others. His emotions shimmered with grief, understanding, and respect for Gregory's sacrifice.

Bro. Simon's voice echoed in their minds. *There's nothing to be ashamed of.*

Not at all, Cedric agreed. *I understand how you feel, man. Like, completely.*

Sophie squeezed Marcus' hand as he blinked a tear onto his cheek.

Our hearts can't help but love the goodness we see in others, she soothed. *Don't be ashamed of it. Embrace it. That's what brings out more of it.*

Marcus glanced at her sidelong. His emotions twisted with confusion and self-doubt, but as he looked at his friends, who smiled at him encouragingly, his emotions calmed.

He sighed and nodded. "None of this makes any sense," he said aloud. "I don't guess it's meant to."

"Nope." Cedric shook his head. "If there's one thing I've learned from all this, it's to not expect it to make any sense. Maybe one day it will, but not today. It's just gonna have to be okay for now."

CHAPTER FIVE

On the last day of April, a week before graduation, she and Marcus headed to Roscoe's workshop for more of the ointment. To Sophie's surprise, Roscoe met them at the workshop door with a mysterious smile.

"Keep your voices down," he urged. Then he let them inside. The workshop was unusually dark. Princess' nearly grown kittens rubbed against Sophie's and Marcus' legs and mewed as they stepped into the kitchen. In a far corner, Sophie heard the tiny squeak of a newborn kitten crying for its mama. Then Princess was at Marcus' feet, her paws up on his knee, begging for petting.

"Oh, my gosh, girl." Marcus chuckled and scratched the mama cat's gold ears affectionately. "You had *more?*"

"I wanna see!" Sophie squealed quietly.

"Come on, you lot. They're about a week old." Roscoe beckoned them to the corner behind his dining room table, where he'd laid a large dog bed. Four tiny balls of fur tumbled around on the soft bed, hunting for Princess. Their eyes were barely open. "Princess went into labor right here in the workshop. You know who's not mad this time?"

Marcus chuckled and patted Roscoe's shoulder. "They're safer here than anywhere else."

Sophie knelt and stretched her hand out toward a gold one, who sniffed it and bobbed its little head in confusion. She noticed they were the same colors as the last litter and shot Princess a knowing look. "Roscoe, you ought to find that gray tabby, wherever he is, and have a little kitty wedding. Clearly, they're meant to be."

"Actually, he hangs out in the barn. He doesn't want to be in that forest right now, either." Roscoe rolled his eyes. "Speaking of cats and weddings, I was gonna let you pick one of the new kittens as a playmate for Nate. Since, you know, you're about to graduate and get married."

"This is a new tradition, I guess," Sophie chuckled. "Princess has kittens right before graduation, and one of us takes one." She eyed Marcus. "Think Nate would want another kitty around?"

"Sure. Maybe one that looks like Princess. You know, so we have one that looks like each of us."

Sophie smiled and reached toward the gold kitten, who mewed at her once before making its bobbing way back to Princess for a meal. "Maybe that one."

"Good choice. Been driving me crazy with its meowing," Roscoe muttered.

"I thought you were getting Princess fixed?" Sophie remarked. "What happened to that?"

"It slipped my mind with everything else going on," Roscoe grumbled. "I'm not angry, though."

Sophie chuckled. "Yeah. Me, either." She stroked the kittens with her fingertips as they nursed.

"Princess won't hardly leave the workshop anymore," Roscoe continued. He glanced at the kitchen window. "Been hearing those howls again, but they're getting creepier." He shuddered. "They're also more frequent and getting closer. Like they know what's coming. Like they're baying for blood."

Sophie's smile fell. "Yeah. You're right. They know exactly what or who is coming. They know the battle's going to take place, and there's no hope left of stopping it." She glanced sadly at the mama cat purring contentedly with her kittens. "Best to keep this happy little family safe with you, Roscoe."

"Don't worry. I'm not letting them out of my sight. Not after what happened last time," Roscoe growled.

There was a scratch on the door, and they all turned toward it and fell silent. Sophie's heart rate jumped. What on earth would be pawing at Roscoe's door? All the cats were inside.

She got up slowly and stretched her mental presence toward the door.

An unfamiliar feline presence brightened in her mind, bright yellow-green with fear.

"It's a cat. It wants in," she noted. "It's scared."

Roscoe frowned. "Ah. Maybe the daddy cat. Guess the barn wasn't good enough for him, the little devil."

Sophie nodded, crossed the floor, and gingerly opened the door. Marcus was on her heels.

A charcoal-gray tabby slipped inside, then stared up at her with pretty gray-green eyes. He meowed questioningly, and a picture blossomed in Sophie's mind—Princess and the kittens.

Sophie laughed and shut the door behind him. "Yes, they're here. So, you're the troublemaker behind all these kittens, hmm?"

He meowed again and twined around her legs, purring like mad.

"Well, how can I be mad at you?" She reached down and scratched his ears, then laughed in surprise as he clambered into her lap. "So affectionate. Just like Princess."

"Or you saved his butt, and now he's buttering you up to feed him," Roscoe grumbled. "Hope you're gonna help pay for his kibble."

"Aw, come on, Roscoe," Sophie teased. "Look at this face." The cat's sleepy eyes were half-closed; he was as happy as a king. Roscoe grumbled something about vet bills while Sophie chuckled and brought the tom to his family. He gingerly sniffed the kittens, then Princess, then curled up behind her to lick her ears.

"Aww." Sophie's eyes welled with tears. "Look at them. They're precious. Should we name the dad?"

"How about Rogue?" Marcus suggested with a smirk. "Since he's apparently very good at sweeping Princess off her feet."

Sophie giggled. "Good idea."

"Once you name it, you get attached to it," Roscoe scolded as he bottled the potion for the tree. "I didn't sign up to be cat foster dad of the year, so if you insist on coddling them, you're gonna take them home with you."

"We might end up with a whole family if we're not

careful, Soph." Marcus chuckled. "Mama, Papa, and the whole kit and caboodle. Literally."

"We can start on that in a couple of months, *mon cher*." Sophie batted her eyelashes at Marcus.

He snorted a shocked laugh, his eyes wide and his cheeks red. "Sophie!"

"Oh, geez," Roscoe groaned and facepalmed. "Take your potion and go. Just 'cause you're getting married doesn't mean anybody else wants to hear your shameless flirting."

Sophie and Marcus didn't quit laughing until they were outside with the jar of ointment.

"I needed that laugh," Marcus admitted as he wiped his eyes. "Oh, goodness. Sometimes you pop off with stuff that shocks the crap out of me."

Sophie chuckled. "It's fun from time to time, you know. Just to remind you who you're dealing with." She winked.

"Do you really want a big family one day?" Marcus asked after a moment of amiable quiet.

Sophie blushed. "Maybe. I only had one sister, and I kind of wish I'd had more siblings."

"I never had any siblings," Marcus noted. He twined his fingers through hers. "I think I want more than one kid at some point."

Sophie's blush reached her ears. "This is so weird."

"Well, *you* brought it up, Miss Confidence," Marcus teased. "Besides, isn't that kind of what married people do? Raise families and go explore the world together?"

"Yeah." Her smile faded as they got closer to Thicket Hall. "Hopefully, the world our future kids grow up in will be a lot safer than this one."

He squeezed her hand, and his magic swirled with firm

determination. "It will be because we're going to make it that way."

Sophie nodded. She thought about Princess and her kittens, hiding in Roscoe's workshop, unable to live their lives. She thought about Millie, who'd never see Thicket Hall in its full glory as a student, and about all the non-magicals who depended on them so they could live their normal lives.

Then she breathed deeply and squeezed his hand back. "Darn right, we are."

At work the next morning, Marcus plunked the handset down and scribbled a laundry list of times and dates on his calendar. He'd just gotten off the phone with EBI agencies in Tennessee and Ohio, who'd promised him a couple of hundred agents in the next few weeks. He hoped it would be enough and that they'd get here before the Serpent did. His case had become the nation's top priority, and he didn't relish the feeling that all eyes looked to him and Trevor to pull off the save of a century. Perhaps several centuries, if Caleb's legendarium about the Defenders was to be believed.

He glanced at the legendarium, a leather-bound monster of a book that spanned nearly his entire desktop. He'd hauled the dusty old book up to his office and had glanced through a few things between visits to the school and escorting Sophie around campus. What he'd found seemed interesting, but what help it offered them as far as practicalities remained to be seen.

He'd made some important notes, though, and he hoped that by combing through it with Cedric's help, they'd be able to piece together a strategy for taking Azdaja down for good.

Apparently, the last time the Serpent had risen from the Realm of Chaos was the first time the Defenders had been chosen and convened. According to his scribbled notes in the margins, Caleb had believed that the channels, as well as their guardians, chose the potential Defenders of each generation. They weren't always needed, and not all Defenders responded to the call. Some generations went by with no recorded Defenders stepping forward to claim their titles, but the role seemed to flow through families of power among the elementals.

That explained why Marcus and Cedric had been chosen. They could trace their Defender "lineage" back to an immediate family member. It also explained Olivia's role since the Wrights had been notably powerful for generations.

What about Sophie, Janet, and Simon? Caleb had painstakingly drawn the family trees of Defender "clusters," patterns of the role that appeared multiple times within certain families and seemed to signal a preference on the part of the guardians for particular lineages. According to that data, the Briggs, Green, and Humphries families were so-called "first generation" Defenders. There had been no previous mention of their families on either father's or mother's side in any of the research Caleb had compiled.

Then again, it seemed that, at least in Sophie's case, she'd been singled out by the most important guardian,

Thicket Hall, from the moment she'd set foot on campus. Was it possible that Thicket Hall had also chosen Simon and Janet for their strength and devotion to their friends like it had chosen Sophie?

Entirely possible. After all, the grumpy old oak had repeatedly advised them that together, they were unstoppable.

He smiled and took a sip of the coffee Dottie had left him. An email popped up on his computer, and his smile dropped.

His honeymoon cabin rental had just been canceled.

"Fantastic," he muttered. He opened the email and skimmed the canned apology, noting that they'd refunded his entire deposit. "They'd better." He hopped onto the rental website and desperately clicked through the dates, trying to find another opening for their honeymoon dates. Unsurprisingly, all but the most expensive cabins had been snatched up for the summer.

He sighed in frustration. It had been his goal to rent them a cozy little cabin for their week away from it all, similar to the one they'd stayed in with the Wrights but smaller and far less expensive. He massaged his temples, trying to think of an alternative. There were plenty of hotels, but that wasn't going to cut it. He wanted something special, something tucked away and peaceful so they could relax and unwind.

Then a memory of vacationing with the Briggs family on Lake Cumberland surfaced. They'd had an RV. They'd been able to take it almost anywhere they wanted, and it had been cozy and private, not to mention cheaper than any of the hotels available for the week of their honeymoon.

Sophie would be able to go on vacation—her first official adult vacation with her new husband—in a familiar, cozy, home-like atmosphere. It was a perfect idea, and hopefully, it would help settle her nerves.

He picked up his phone and dialed Walter, Sophie's dad.

"Hey, son." Walter's normally cheerful voice was tempered with concern. "Everything okay?"

"Yeah, yeah. Sophie's fine. I just had a question for you," Marcus explained. "Mine and Sophie's honeymoon cabin just got canceled, and I was wondering if we could borrow the Briggs RV for the week instead?" He chuckled nervously. "Obviously, I'd take good care of it. I just figured it would be nice for her to have something familiar. You know, being out on her own for the first time."

"Hmm." Walter paused, then chuckled. "It's a good thing you're marrying into the Briggs family. Any other young lady would laugh in your face if you told her your first vacation together was gonna be in a thirty-year-old RV out in the woods."

Marcus laughed. "Yeah. I'm a lucky guy." He glanced at the photo of Sophie on his desk with a tender smile.

"I think your intuition is spot-on, though, son," Walter continued. "For all its creaks and leaks, Sophie loves our RV. I think she'd be thrilled to take it on her first grown-up vacation. Just make sure you practice backing up," Walter added with a conspiratorial undertone. "Thing has a turning radius of the Grand Canyon."

"Noted, Mr. Briggs…I mean, Walter." Marcus caught himself with a laugh. "I definitely appreciate it."

"No problem, son. You take care."

Marcus set his phone down and grinned at the photo of Sophie. No need to plunk down his refunded deposit to impress the girl he loved. He'd been able to turn this seeming defeat into a resounding victory for him and Sophie and for their bank account, even amid the chaos they were living in.

Hope sparked like a flame in his heart.

"We're gonna have the time of our lives, babe." He kissed his fingers and touched Sophie's photo. "I promise."

CHAPTER SIX

Sophie stood in the girls' bathroom for the last time on the first Saturday in May, choking back tears. Leslie, Bri, Janet, Charlotte, and Olivia stood beside her, getting ready alongside her.

"I see that look, Miracle Grow," Olivia scolded as she shook out her curled hair in the mirror. "If you cry, you're gonna make us all cry, dang it."

Sophie chuckled. "I can't help it, Liv. After today, we won't be students anymore." Her voice broke.

Janet's lip curled into a pout just as Bri moved to apply her lipstick, creating a pink smear on her chin.

"Sophie!" Bri swatted her friend playfully, then scrubbed Janet's chin with a makeup wipe. "Now look what you've done."

Sophie laughed. "Sorry."

Leslie sighed as she put the finishing touches on her makeup. "Man, I'm really gonna miss this place, y'all."

"We have to hang out this summer," Charlotte put in.

"Maybe Miss Money over here can fund another trip to Gatlinburg." She grinned at Olivia, who rolled her eyes.

"Maybe so."

"Sophie's already going with *Marcus*," teased Bri. She bumped her hip into Sophie's and wiggled her eyebrows. "All alone together for the first time ever."

Sophie blushed. "He'll be my *husband* at that point, Bri. That's a totally normal thing." She turned back to her mascara, cursing the heat in her cheeks.

"Mmhmm," Charlotte teased. "I tell you what else will be normal. Won't nobody be able to get ahold of y'all."

Olivia and Bri and Charlotte cackled as Sophie's blush rose clear to her ears.

"We're just teasing," Olivia soothed. She stood behind Sophie and curled a strand of her hair through her fingers. Her eyes lit up red-orange, and Sophie watched as a perfect curl replaced the shoddy one Sophie had created with the curling iron.

Don't let our teasing get to you, Miss Angel, Liv told Sophie in her mind. *You guys will have a great time. If I've learned anything about Prince Death over the years, it's that you're a goddess in his mind. He adores you, and he'd never do anything to hurt you.*

"Thanks, Liv." Sophie gave Olivia a meaningful smile, and the taller girl stepped away with a wink.

Sophie finished her makeup, then fastened her graduation cap on her head and donned her hunter-green graduation gown over the blue dress she'd chosen for the ceremony.

"We're officially graduating," she told her reflection.

Janet slipped an arm around her waist, looking adorable with her long brown hair curled around her face. "We're adults now. It's gonna be exciting and stressful, but I hope we all stick together after this."

"Ditto, girl." Sophie squeezed Janet in a side hug, then patted her cheek affectionately. "Let's go meet the guys, shall we?"

Janet, Sophie, and Olivia met their EBI escorts in the lobby of the girls' dorm. Marcus was Sophie's, and Cedric was Olivia's. Janet and Simon walked arm in arm, flanked by Agents Colton and Wright. Agent Wright, Olivia's mom, kissed her daughter's forehead and squeezed her before waving goodbye as Cedric swept her outside.

"Glad I get to be here with you today," Marcus told Sophie as he walked her outside. They met the Briggs family just up the sidewalk. Sophie's mother and father and sister flanked the two of them with proud smiles and hugs.

"I'm glad you're here, too," Sophie replied. "We're strong, but having everyone here with me makes me feel much stronger."

"We're better together," Marcus noted.

Sophie squeezed Marcus' arm. She wasn't supposed to show tons of affection to him when he was in uniform, but she couldn't help it. It *was* a special day and also the anniversary of their engagement.

"Darn right we are," she replied with a radiant grin.

Marcus faced forward with his prim and proper work attitude, but his emotions swelled with love, pride, and hope.

With her last name at the beginning of the alphabet, it didn't take long until it was Sophie's moment to shine after the ceremony started.

"Sophia Joy Briggs," called Headmistress Rogers, and to Sophie's shock, her entire class stood and applauded as Marcus led her to the platform.

"That's my girl!" Charlotte, Bri, Leslie, Janet, and Olivia shouted from their seats as she passed.

Sophie laughed, and her eyes filled with tears of gratitude.

"Watch your step, princess." Marcus helped her up the narrow steps, then took his place with his hands folded in front of him near the foot of the steps on the other side. He gave her an encouraging wink, then faced forward, scanning the crowd for threats.

Sophie smiled at him and shook hands with Headmistress Rogers and Professor Garver, then saw Roscoe and Norma Case at the podium, waiting for her with huge smiles.

"Another little presentation for yet another very special graduate," Norma explained into the microphone. The crowd burst into cheers once more as Sophie covered her mouth with her hands. Roscoe took her arm with a gentle smile and escorted her to the hawkish old woman.

"We wanted to do something special for you since you ain't never stopped taking care of our school since you got here," Roscoe told her.

"It's true that our beloved Thicket Hall will soon leave us," Norma began, speaking into the microphone. The crowd quieted. "However, it won't leave without a fight, and that fight is being waged tirelessly, thanks in large part to the efforts of a very determined and talented young lady."

She studied Sophie with a proud smile. "Sophie, you've brought out the best in all of us time and time again. You've brought us together under a single banner of hope, and we want you to know that we'll follow you and the Defenders to this last battle, come what may."

The crowd roared its agreement, and Sophie bit her lip to keep it from trembling. She didn't deserve all this fuss. She hadn't walked alone through any of it.

Norma pulled something from under the podium. It sparkled in the sunlight and seemed to glow with its own radiance. She pinned it to Sophie's graduation gown, and Sophie gasped as she traced a familiar veiny maple leaf, now encased in a stunning crystal brooch, preserved from the disease coursing through Thicket Hall's boughs.

Very nice, that is, Thicket Hall rumbled from the acorn in her pocket.

Sophie smiled in agreement. She'd treasure it forever.

"Thicket Hall chose you to lead the fight for its life, and it couldn't have chosen better," Roscoe concluded with tears in his eyes. "In honor of the moment it picked you out from the crowd of freshmen four years ago, and as a symbol of our gratitude and loyalty, we want you to have this to treasure as you move into your new life." He leaned away from the microphone and whispered near Sophie's ear, "Also, you're getting a cat from me, so…"

Sophie laughed and wiped her eyes. She looked earnestly at them both and pulled them into a hug.

"Thank you," she told them. "I couldn't have done any of this without you."

"Speech!" The crowd chanted, and Norma gestured at the podium with an arched eyebrow.

"Will you indulge them, Miss Briggs?"

"I guess so." She stepped to the microphone, nodding and waving politely, and the crowd cheered.

"Get it!" Charlotte called as everyone quieted. Peter gave an exuberant holler, and Sophie chuckled when she saw Marcus crack a smile near the foot of the stairs.

"Thanks for that welcome, guys," she teased. She gazed at the crowd, her throat suddenly dry. What was she going to say? She took a deep breath and touched the brooch on her gown. "I just wanted everyone to know that the Defenders and I can't do this without you. We could not have done *any* of it without you. You are *all superheroes.*"

She paused as smiles bloomed in the crowd like spring flowers. "You gathered around us from the very beginning. You came to mine and Marcus' rescue dozens of times when you didn't have to." Her eyes paused on Mikey and Sabrina, who beamed at her, then traveled to Charlotte, Peter, and the rest of her roommates, who sat hugging each other and dabbing their cheeks with tissues.

"Got that right," Peter snarked to the laughter of the entire crowd.

Sophie laughed as she continued. "Together, we've faced enemies with tremendous power. We've pulled together time and time again to rescue our beloved school from the clutches of evil, and we still have the most dangerous enemy of all to face."

The crowd stilled as her words sobered them.

"I know we can do it again," she encouraged. "I know that if we all pull together, if we rely on each other, and if we keep up our hope, we can do it one last time."

"Yeah!" Mikey pumped his fist, setting off another round of cheers and whoops of affirmation.

"Onward with hope!" Sophie cried, raising her fist. "Onward with love until this final evil is no more!"

The crowd stood and roared its approval and agreement, and Sophie blew a kiss and stepped away from the mic with tears welling in her eyes.

She'd given them hope and encouragement. It would have to be enough. Everything she'd just said was true, and she hoped she wasn't just fooling them all with a deluded vision of victory.

Marcus took her arm as she stepped down from the platform, unable to keep a smile from his face.

That was amazing, babe, he told her. *They'd follow you to hell and back, you know that?*

Sophie sighed. *I know. That's exactly where I* don't *want to lead them, though. As if everything we've been through wasn't enough, we still have one more fight to win. If I'm honest, I'm afraid we won't.*

She avoided his gaze. *What happens if we fail them, Marcus?*

Marcus twined his fingers through hers, and she glanced at him in surprise. He was letting his agent demeanor slip in a big way.

"You're never alone," he murmured. His eyes pierced her. "You never have been, and you've got to remember that. They're here fighting beside you because they want to be, Sophie. You're not leading them anywhere they're not willing to be."

Sophie gazed at him and let the truth of his words sink into her soul. Though it didn't get rid of the dread, a little more light shone in the darkness.

CHAPTER SEVEN

Sophie woke up in her bed at the Briggs home on Monday morning as bright May sunshine filtered through her gauzy pink curtains. She stretched and yawned, then sat for a long moment as her new reality set in.

She was a graduate now, nearly an adult. She would report to her new full-time job today, and she'd never again set foot on the campus of the School of Roots and Vines as a student.

This was the young woman she'd been wondering if she'd become at the ice cream shop with her father what seemed like ages ago. She was here, whether she was ready or not.

Her eyes welled with bittersweet tears, and she touched the crystal leaf Norma and Roscoe had given her, along with the gold acorn she'd placed beside it on her desk.

So this is where you live, sapling, Thicket Hall rumbled, stirring at her touch. *Not as nice as a forest.*

Sophie chuckled. *I like it just fine, you old grump. Here. Have some sunlight.* She got up and pulled the curtains aside, and as the morning sun streamed through onto the acorn, Thicket Hall's presence warmed contentedly in her mind.

Is good, sapling. Soon, soil and water I will need. Janet and Simon help.

Sophie grinned. *For sure.*

Someone knocked gently on her door. "Princess? You awake?" It was Marcus, who'd spent the weekend in the guest room after celebrating her graduation with her family.

"Yeah." Sophie shrugged on one of his old hoodies to cover the tank top she'd slept in. "Come in."

Marcus gingerly pushed open the door and grinned when he saw what she was wearing.

"Makes a great pajama shirt, huh?"

"It sure does," Sophie admitted as she tucked her hands into the large front pockets. "Did you sleep okay?"

"Yeah." Marcus paused near her desk and smiled affectionately at the sunbathing acorn. *How are you doing, little acorn?*

That's majestic oak to you, Thicket Hall snarked.

Marcus chuckled. *Good to know you're as sharp as ever.* He returned his attention to Sophie with a teasing grin. "Well, princess, we'd better get ready for work. Partner agents now and all."

"I think we'll end up like Dottie and Trevor," Sophie noted. "Just like we wanted."

"I think so, too." He pulled something from behind his back—a cube-shaped black box wrapped in silver ribbon. "A little gift for your first official workday, babe."

"Marcus," Sophie scolded playfully, but her heart melted. "You know we're supposed to be saving money."

"We're doing fine," Marcus reassured her. "Once we combine accounts in a couple of months, you won't worry so much about this. Trust me." He winked.

Sophie laughed as she pulled off the ribbon. "Is that your ego I hear?"

"Maybe, but I got a right to be proud of all those zeroes in our savings, okay?"

"Yes, you do." Sophie patted his cheek, then lifted the lid off the box.

The first thing that caught her eye was a badge. Her new work badge? She lifted it out and read the engraving with a smile. *Sophie Briggs, Co-Lead Agent.*

"I like the sound of that," she whispered as she traced the letters. "Are you a co-lead now, too?"

"Of course." Marcus pulled his badge from his wallet and showed it to her, then flashed her a smirk. "When we're married, we'll have to update yours with your new last name."

Sophie blushed fiercely. "Y-yeah."

Marcus laughed and threw an arm around her shoulder. "You're adorable when you're embarrassed." He gestured at her gift. "Go on. There's more."

Sophie pulled out the tissue paper covering the rest of the gift and gasped in delight.

A half-dozen crystal roses sparkled in the sun, arranged in a matching crystal vase. The vase had her name engraved on a silver plate attached to the front.

"For your new desk," he explained. "I'm sure you'll have your African violet and tons of other living plants, but you know. Something to remind you of me."

"They're beautiful," Sophie murmured. She glanced at

the other crystal roses Marcus had given her over the years, sparkling on the desk in her room. "I think I'll bring them all."

Marcus laughed. "You've got a whole dozen now, I think."

Sophie set the gift aside and hugged Marcus. "You sure know how to make a girl feel special."

"I try." He kissed her cheek. "Now, go get ready, beautiful. Let me make you coffee for your first full day of work."

Sophie batted her eyelashes. "Are you always gonna spoil me like this?"

"As often as I can." He gazed at her with affection.

Sophie pulled him close and kissed him gently. "You're amazing. Not just for this but for everything you do. Your overtime work, the way you protect the school and me, and saving money for us and making sure we'll be okay... It all means the world to me. I hope you know that."

Marcus hugged her, and Sophie felt his emotions swirling happily. "All I want is to make you happy. You deserve the world, Sophie."

"So do you." They gazed at each other for a long moment, and Sophie's heart brimmed with affection and confidence.

Then her alarm buzzed, and Marcus' eyes widened with excitement.

"If we sit here telling each other how much we love each other all morning, we'll never get to work on time." He headed for the door. "We'll have to remember that when we're married."

Sophie laughed and kissed his cheek. "Meet you for breakfast in a few, babe."

A half-hour later, Sophie sat at the Briggs dining room table with a cup of coffee and a plate of eggs, dressed in her official black EBI jumpsuit. She'd pulled her hair into a cute high ponytail, and her makeup was minimal yet polished. She'd looked like a real agent when she saw her reflection in the bathroom mirror. She was thrilled, but she still felt like a child in an adult costume.

She supposed it would take time to get used to all this.

"I got it, Mrs. Briggs…I mean, Joyce," Marcus insisted as Sophie's mother brought their waffles to the table. "I didn't mean for you to have to come in here and fuss over us."

"What's a mother have to do if she doesn't fuss over her kids?" Joyce laughed. "Go sit down."

Marcus, also in his black uniform with his blond hair neatly pulled back, sat next to Sophie with a resigned smile. "I can't get her to take a day off," he whispered to Sophie.

Sophie chuckled. "That's Mom for you."

As they ate in amiable silence, Walter stepped into the kitchen with a stretch and a yawn, then eyed them in their uniforms.

"Well, well, look at you two," he teased with a crinkly smile. "All official and whatnot."

Sophie grinned. "I'm not used to it either, Dad." She glanced around questioningly. "Where's Mills? She said she wanted to see us off."

"You know how teenagers are," Walter sighed. "She'll probably sleep until eleven, then demand we take her to see you."

"Sounds about right," Marcus quipped. His phone chirped at the same time as Sophie's, and they glanced at one another, then checked Trevor's message.

Happy first day, Sophie. Unfortunately, it's gonna be a long one for you and your co-lead. We need you to work a ten instead of an eight. A stomach bug broke out on campus this weekend and took out a lot of our help among the faculty. Think you can swing it?

Marcus sighed. "Well, that's great. First day, and they already need us to work overtime. I'm used to it, but I didn't want you to have to do it, too."

Sophie smiled grimly. "I get the feeling this is gonna happen a lot over the next few weeks."

Marcus sipped his coffee. "Most likely."

"Welcome to adulthood, Soph." Walter patted her back comfortingly. "Fun, isn't it?"

Joyce rolled her eyes. "Don't let him tease you. It's hard sometimes, but I know the two of you can handle it just fine. We'll be right here to support you." She patted their shoulders. "You'd better hurry if you want to get there on time."

"Wait!" Millie hurried into the kitchen, hair disheveled and pajamas wrinkled. She tackled Marcus and Sophie in a hug. "Good luck today, sissy."

Sophie hugged her back with a laugh. "Goodness, Mills. Did you just now wake up?"

"Look, it's 8 AM. I'm not ready to start my day until at least noon," Millie snarked.

"You'll have to get up earlier than that for classes this fall," Marcus reminded her as he ruffled her hair.

"Don't remind me." Millie shuffled over to the coffee pot and rubbed her eyes while Marcus and Sophie laughed.

A bit later, Sophie slipped into the passenger seat of Marcus' car, and they headed to the school.

"So weird to be going back but not going back," Sophie noted.

"I know, right?" Marcus slipped on his aviators, and with his slicked-back hair and black uniform, Sophie was vividly reminded of Gregory Templeton. She preferred Marcus' looser, more punky style to the suave, business-like persona he had to adopt for work.

Then again, maybe Gregory Templeton had been like Marcus in his younger years and had only become the slick, no-nonsense EA President Sophie knew him as over time, as adulthood—and the responsibility of a cursed family—weighed him down.

Either way, the stern-looking young man next to her sent a shiver down her spine.

"Let's jam," she told him quietly.

"Why? Nervous?" He flashed her a grin, which helped tear down his strange façade.

"No." Sophie fidgeted nervously, unsure if she should tell him what she'd been thinking. "I just want to enjoy the ride."

"You know we have to get used to being around each

other at work, Soph," Marcus reminded her gently. "We can't be all doe-eyed while we're on the job."

"I know, babe." Sophie crossed her arms and stared out the window.

Marcus coaxed her arm loose and took her hand. "I didn't say that to make you mad." He squeezed her fingers. "I can sense something's bothering you."

Sophie sighed. She wasn't going to be able to hide it from him. "You're all adult now, Marcus. I don't know how to deal with it yet. Every day, it seems like you're less of the carefree, romantic, punky guy I fell in love with and more of this strong, silent, responsible type. Don't get me wrong, it's not a bad thing, the ways that you're changing. Just, it sometimes makes me...I don't know. Uncomfortable." She squirmed. "Like, I don't know you as well as I think."

Marcus rubbed his thumb across the back of her hand, and Sophie felt his emotions stir thoughtfully in his magic. "Princess, even if we're on the job, even if we have to use this persona to do what needs to get done, I still love you. I would still die for you, and *nothing* about our love changes, okay?"

"I know that. I feel the same," Sophie protested. She straightened and looked at him sheepishly. "When I see you like this, though, I see..." Her voice trailed off, but the way Marcus frowned told her he'd seen her thoughts and felt the truth in her emotions.

"I've been thinking a lot about that lately," he told her quietly. "I feel like I understand him a lot more. I understand why he is the way he is. He was thrown into all this so fast. It's had a similar effect on me as far as chilling me out and making me less likely to take risks and more likely to strategize."

His voice was tight and determined. "Just because I say I understand him, and though there might be similarities in the way we look and think, it doesn't excuse any of the bad things he's done. It also doesn't mean *I'm* going to become a villain."

"Of course not," Sophie reassured him. It was her turn to squeeze his hand. "I just worry for you, as in your mental and emotional health. I don't want you to shut down or forget why we're fighting so hard." She gulped. "I don't want to lose the person I fell in love with in the midst of all this chaos."

Marcus lifted her hand to his lips and kissed it. "*Cara mia*, I'm not going anywhere. I can promise you that." His lips curled in an irresistible smirk. "We have to tone it down when we work together, but once we're off the clock, I can be as carefree and romantic as you want."

Sophie blushed. "I guess that's true."

Marcus winked and gave her one of his lopsided smiles.

CHAPTER EIGHT

They reached the campus. Sophie's lip trembled when she saw the budding pear trees, the headmistress' garden, and Thicket Hall's familiar towering form. She patted the acorn in her pocket.

Sad you are, sapling. Can sense it.

I'm not a sapling anymore, Sophie replied sadly. *I'm not a student. I'm an agent now, and this is my life.*

Good, it is. Thicket Hall chuckled. *Cannot stay sapling forever. Mighty oak, you must become.*

Sophie smiled. *You always know what to say, old friend.*

Been around for almost eight hundred years, I have, Thicket Hall retorted. *Should know good things to say by now.*

Marcus, who'd been walking beside her, chuckled and squeezed her hand. "Thicket Hall is right. You can't stay a baby forever, but it doesn't mean your light dims. It gets bigger and brighter."

Sophie nodded. "Thanks, guys." Her phone blipped, and a text from Charlotte blinked onto the screen.

You on campus yet? Need you at Nurse Bonnie's place. This stomach bug is killer!

Sophie frowned. "Is that where Trevor wants me?"

"He's not picky. As long as you're here and you can document what you did for the day, it all counts," Marcus told her.

"What are you gonna do?"

"Simon told me there's some decay I need to take care of under Thicket Hall's roots," Marcus explained with a grimace. "Nasty stuff, but it's like cleaning a wound. Necessary."

Sophie nodded and paused at the break in the path behind Thicket Hall. "I guess this is where we part ways, *mon cher.*"

"I'll see you at lunch. 12:30. Not a minute later." *You'll get a kiss then,* he told her in her mind.

Sophie blushed and grinned shyly. *Deal.* She wiggled her fingers in a goodbye wave, then headed to the charming house where Nurse Bonnie tended the student population. Its yellow siding and teeming front gardens brought back good memories, and Sophie sighed as she struggled to come to grips with all the emotions she felt. She stepped onto the front porch and opened the door. The bell tinkled overhead, and the familiar scents of vanilla and cinnamon washed over her as she stepped inside.

"Soph? Is that you, girl?" Charlotte peeked out of the infirmary with her nose and mouth covered by a mask. She tossed Sophie a wrapped one. "Here. You're gonna need this."

Sophie put the mask on as dread gripped her. She

followed Charlotte into the infirmary, where a dozen faculty members lay pale and trembling on the beds.

"Goodness," she whispered. "So many."

"This bug came out of nowhere," Nurse Bonnie explained as she bustled to Professor Welby's side with a can of ginger ale. "It's got everyone out of sorts, and it's not a simple twenty-four-hour bug like most stomach viruses. It'll last a couple of days, then stop, then come back again a day later. I can't make heads or tails of it."

She shook her head. "We've needed to buy more anti-nausea medication, in addition to wearing ourselves out using life energy to keep up their strength. They can't work or heal if they can't keep food down."

Sophie's brow furrowed. This had all the hallmarks of an attack, not an accident. The enemy knew they were trying to delay the Serpent's coming by using all their resources to keep Thicket Hall alive. Was it possible Azdaja or her servants could have concocted a superbug to put their forces out of commission?

She examined the faces on the cots and found Garver and Tuttle among them. Each was a professor with elemental magic who'd been pouring their resources into Thicket Hall's salvation. Not a single custodian, kitchen worker, or groundskeeper had been affected.

She went over to Garver, who smiled weakly at her.

"Hey there, Miss Brand New Agent," Garver teased. She coughed, and her face went pale. "Oh, no. Not again."

Sophie put her hand on Garver's forehead and sent a gentle burst of life energy through her, calming her nausea. Garver took several deep breaths and gulped, then nodded. "Thanks for that."

"No problem. Do you mind if I examine you?"

"Go right ahead," Garver croaked. "I don't know if you'll find anything Nurse Bonnie and Charlotte didn't, but it's worth a shot."

Sophie nodded, then closed her eyes and let her magic probe Garver's body.

Garver stiffened. "Yeesh, this is creepy."

"Sorry." Sophie chuckled. "I'm trying to figure out if this bug is natural or magical."

"Oh," Nurse Bonnie murmured. "You know, I hadn't thought of that. I always assume it's natural. Very few magical illnesses are around anymore."

Sophie's life energy returned after a thorough pass of Garver, carrying a lone speck of telltale death and earth magic. As soon as it passed into her hands, Sophie clamped a hand over her mouth against sudden urgent nausea.

"Bingo," she croaked.

Working quickly to stave off the urge to vomit, she separated the earth and death magic with some effort. It resisted her fiercely for such a small amount of magic. Then she passed the earth magic into her right hand and the death magic into her left.

"Girl, you working some kind of voodoo over there?" Charlotte snarked.

"Phenomenal," Tuttle rasped. "Truly remarkable."

Garver sighed in relief. "I feel much better already."

Sophie opened her eyes. Her hands were tinted emerald on the right and charcoal-gray on the left, and everyone in the room was staring at her in shock.

She chuckled nervously. "Excuse me for a second. I need to get rid of this."

"Allow me." Tuttle reached for her left hand, and the death magic passed to him. His eyes flashed silver.

"I could take the earth magic," Welby offered from across the room. Sophie hurried over and gave it to him, and her magic was clear again. She turned to find Nurse Bonnie and Charlotte checking Garver.

"I promise I feel normal," Garver insisted as they fussed over her. "Starving, though." Her stomach growled, punctuating her point.

Sophie put a hand on Charlotte's and Nurse Bonnie's shoulders. "Let her eat. She should be fine. The bug is magical, as I suspected. It's a mix of earth and death magic I've seen before." She shuddered, remembering the rock creature. "The nausea stops when I separate the elements."

"Interesting." Nurse Bonnie tapped her chin. "Do you think you can get everyone back on their feet without wearing yourself out?"

Sophie nodded. "If you've got plenty of food on hand, I've got all day."

Lunchtime arrived, and Sophie's head spun, and her stomach howled with hunger. She had gotten through nearly all the patients in Nurse Bonnie's office, and despite the plethora of potato chips and bananas she'd eaten, she needed more.

The bell jingled, and Marcus stepped in. He took one look at Sophie, and his eyes widened.

"Princess. You look like death."

She flashed him a grim smile. "Yeah, but *they* don't feel

like death anymore." She jerked her thumb at the infirmary, where the faculty she'd just healed were being inspected a final time and then released by Charlotte and Nurse Bonnie.

He chuckled and wrapped an arm around her waist to steady her. "What you need is about five cups of the school's famous coffee."

"Do they have any made?" Sophie asked hopefully.

"Indeed they do." He tugged her forward, and she wobbled. "Need me to carry you?"

"I wouldn't mind that," Sophie teased breathlessly. Then vertigo overtook her, and she shut her eyes and leaned against him. "Goodness."

"Come on, sweetheart." Marcus scooped her up and tucked her against his chest. "I always end up doing this for some reason," he teased.

Sophie hugged his neck and kept her eyes closed as he carried her to Thicket Hall. "Reminds me of the good old days," she mumbled.

Marcus laughed through his nose. "I know, right?"

"Hey, Prince Death. She okay?"

Sophie heard Olivia's question and opened her eyes. Her vision spun, but she tried to flash Olivia a thumbs-up.

"She'll be fine once she gets some coffee," Marcus soothed. "Wore herself out this morning."

"That's just like you, Miss Miracles." Olivia scolded. "I better see you back in action after lunch, you hear me?"

"Yes, ma'am." Sophie gave her a weak salute and let her head fall back on Marcus' shoulder.

When they entered Thicket Hall's dining area, he set

her down gently at their old table, which was vacant for the summer.

"You sit tight. I'll be back with a banquet." He winked, kissed her cheek, and headed to the kitchen.

"Hey there, Miss Agent."

Sophie glanced up wearily and smiled as Peter, Simon, and Janet joined her at the table.

"You guys at lunch, too?"

"I'm always at lunch," Peter quipped. "Ain't got my first official job yet, so I'm hanging around with you weirdos in black suits."

Sophie laughed. "Pete."

"You look pale, Sophie." Janet put a hand on her forehead.

"Just doing too much, as usual," Sophie snarked. "Marcus went to get me some food and coffee."

"Ooh, coffee." Janet drummed her fingers on the table in delight. "I could use some of that." She batted her eyelashes at Simon. "Would you be a dear?"

Simon rolled his eyes, but he got up. "Sure thing, babe."

"Oh, my gosh." An unfamiliar voice made Sophie turn. A teen girl stood in front of their table, looking like she might burst from excitement. "Are you Sophie Briggs?"

Sophie smiled politely. "Yeah."

The girl squealed. "I've been following your adventures for, like, ever. Big fan."

Sophie laughed in disbelief. "Adventures?"

"You know, like the time you broke into Darla Templeton's office, and the time you came back to life after Gregory Templeton almost killed you, and the time you and all your friends kicked Connor's butt after he tried to make this school into a magical factory." As she spoke, she flipped through a handmade book with newspaper clippings and photos from online news sites, showing Sophie each incident.

"Oh. I see." Sophie laughed. "Wow. I didn't know we were celebrities, guys." She glanced at her friends, who chuckled.

"I'll be a first-year next year. Been helping with the efforts to save Thicket Hall, you know." She held out her hand for Sophie to shake. "I'm Emily, by the way. Emily Frederickson. I have life, too."

"It's good to meet you, Emily," Sophie greeted.

A plate was set in front of her, and she glanced up with a grateful smile as Marcus sat next to her.

Emily squealed. "Oh, gosh. Is that Marcus?"

Marcus glanced at the girl in surprise and gave her a polite smile. "Um. Hi."

Emily dissolved into nervous giggles. "Sorry! Sorry. I'm fan-girling hard right now."

Sophie chuckled and turned to Marcus. "Apparently, we're celebrities. Marcus, this is Emily. She's an incoming first-year who's here to help Thicket Hall."

"Nice to meet you, Em." Marcus held out his hand, and Emily shook it nervously. "We appreciate you coming on your summer break to help with the cause."

"Of course," Emily gushed. "I want there to still *be* a school when I start classes in the fall."

"Totally agree," Janet put in. "Sophie, isn't your sister going to start in the fall, too?"

"Yep. She'll be in your class, Emily. Her name is Amelia, but she goes by Millie. Also life, of course."

Emily gasped. "Oh, wow! That'll be amazing!" She danced in a circle. "You think I could get her number?"

"Sure. She'd love to have a friend when she gets here." Sophie took Emily's phone and put Millie's number in.

"I think she and Mills will get along like peas in a pod," Marcus remarked with a chuckle.

"They have the same level of enthusiasm," Janet added.

"Wait." Emily studied Janet, and her eyes widened with delight. "You're the girl who stopped Connor by turning into a solid wall of rock."

Simon, who'd just come back to the table, patted Janet's back with an affectionate grin.

"She sure is. And I'm the guy she saved."

Janet swatted him playfully while Emily giggled.

CHAPTER NINE

Two weeks of full-time and often overtime work for Sophie passed in an exhausting haze. She managed to keep the Serpent's unnatural stomach bug at bay, and Marcus and the other Defenders, plus a few zealous students and Garver, Tuttle, and the rest of the faculty, worked like mad to keep the remainder of Thicket Hall's leaves green and shiny. Half had turned rust-red and dropped to the ground, giving the illusion of autumn in the midst of spring.

Tree needs you too, sapling, Thicket Hall told Sophie after a shift of caring for the exhausted and sick in Nurse Bonnie's infirmary. *Feeling I have that enemy trying to divide you on purpose.*

I know, Sophie replied as she patted her pocket, her eyes heavy and her stomach growling. *It's better for me to make sure every able person is healthy, though. Even if I'm a Defender, I'm only one life elemental. The more power we put into you, the better.*

She met Marcus inside the dining hall, where the familiar gleaming oak walls seemed a little less lustrous in the cheerful late-May sun streaming through the windows. He'd gotten a plate of food and a cup of coffee for her, and he gave her a grim smile as she sat down next to him with a sigh.

"Rough day, huh?" He shook his hair loose. They were off the clock.

Sophie nodded and mutely tucked into her food.

"I'll wait to ask you until you've eaten," Marcus noted with a chuckle. He rubbed her back as she silently filled her tummy.

"Okay." Sophie sighed once her stomach quit growling, then patted her mouth with a napkin. "What did you want to ask me?"

Marcus pulled a navy-blue envelope out of his jacket and handed it to Sophie. She recognized the sun and moon seal as the ones she'd picked out for their wedding invitations.

"An invitation? Did I forget to send one?" She turned the envelope over, but there were no addresses on the front. She gave Marcus a quizzical look.

He didn't meet her gaze. "I was going to ask you. Are you comfortable with the Templetons attending our wedding?"

Sophie blinked as her heart twisted. "Can they even do that? They're in jail."

Marcus nodded slowly. "I, um, I asked Trevor if they could come. You know, heavily guarded, with elemental restraints. The whole shebang. He pulled some strings at the prison to arrange for them to be there, and I felt I should ask you now that I know it's a possibility."

Sophie glanced at the invitation dubiously. They'd been

planning on going to visit the Templetons today and digging for more answers from Gregory since, in person, they'd have more than five minutes to speak. She'd bet anything he intended to give them this invitation.

"Marcus," Sophie began. She reached for his hand and squeezed it.

He looked away uncertainly. "It's totally cool if you say no. I understand *completely*. I probably shouldn't have even pushed for it, but—"

"Marcus." Sophie took his face in her hands. "Hey. Look at me."

Marcus met her gaze with a vulnerable look she hadn't seen since the day he'd asked to sit at her friends' table.

She smiled tenderly. "I'm totally comfortable with it, babe. It's important to you, and honestly, it's important to me, too. I'm glad you were able to work it out."

His eyes widened in surprise. "It's important to you? How? I mean, Gregory almost…" His voice trailed off as Sophie shook her head.

"I never held your past against you after you proved you were never going down that path again. Gregory has done the same thing. He's saved my life *three* times, and Darla? Well." Sophie chuckled. "She doesn't approve of me, but she loves *you* with all her heart and wants to make things right. That's all I could ask of them, especially now that they're facing justice for what they've done. It's the best ending we could hope for."

Marcus' fearful expression morphed into understanding and hope as Sophie spoke. He pulled her into a hug.

"You don't know what this means to me, Sophie. Heck, *I* don't even understand why it means so much to me."

Sophie chuckled and ran her fingers through his long hair. "Love works in strange ways, Marcus. It's never wrong to love the good in people, babe. *Never.*"

They stepped through the metal detectors at the high-security prison where the Templetons were being held. Sophie shifted nervously as she pinned her EBI badge back on her uniform and took Marcus' arm.

"It's down this way," the guard said. Marcus strode down a long corridor after him, and as they reached a set of double doors, he scanned the security key given to him by the guard. They opened onto another corridor. Sophie could tell by the spacing of the doors and the way the hall hummed with elemental energy that this was a containment wing.

"There." Marcus pointed at a door at the end of the hall and double-checked the sticky note. "Cell 505."

As they approached the door, a white-clad guard stopped them and looked at their clearance papers.

"Twenty minutes," the guard reminded them. Then he opened the door and led them into a bare room with a wide plexiglass window covered by a metal security door. Two chairs were pulled close to the glass, and as Sophie and Marcus sat, the metal door rose, revealing who sat on the other side of the plexiglass.

Sophie produced a polite smile as Gregory and Darla greeted them with grim smiles of their own. They were dressed in white jumpsuits and had semi-permanent elemental restraints on their wrists.

Marcus gulped. "Um. Hi."

Sophie gripped his hand comfortingly.

Darla cracked an affectionate smile. "Hello, darling." Her voice was mechanical and reedy through a small speaker near the center of the plexiglass.

Gregory nodded at them, his amber eyes glimmering. Then he cleared his throat. "It's good to see you both this evening."

Marcus glanced sidelong at Sophie, and she gave him an encouraging smile.

"I assume you are here to give me an update on the status of Thicket Hall?" Gregory continued.

Marcus nodded. "Yeah. It's not doing great."

Gregory arched an eyebrow. "Has it fallen?"

"No," Sophie answered. "It's lost a lot of its leaves. It's like a tree in the fall, dropping red leaves everywhere. We're doing all we can, but I've had to deal with a magical sickness that's put everyone out of commission, so I haven't been able to help much."

"That's not good," Gregory responded, scratching his stubbly chin. "You are the life Defender. You should be helping strengthen the tree. What is the nature of this illness you've been healing?"

"It's a mix of earth and death magic, something we've seen before with you-know-what's zombie creatures," Marcus responded. "Sophie is the only one who can separate elemental magic, and that's the only way to get rid of it. She's been working herself to death trying to keep everyone well."

Gregory's eyes flashed. "Which is exactly what the enemy wants."

Marcus and Sophie nodded.

Gregory exchanged worried glances with Darla. "I fear there might only be one recourse left. Thicket Hall's fall is inevitable, and it will happen sooner rather than later if Miss Briggs continues to have to deal with the distraction of the illness," Gregory explained. He gazed at them, and Sophie could almost see the gears turning in his head as his eyes narrowed. "You must gather your army *now*. Act as if the enemy is coming tomorrow. Waste no time. As soon as it's reasonably possible, set the date for the final battle. Preferably after your wedding, but if it must be sooner, so be it." He glanced apologetically at Marcus before he continued. "Then you must take Thicket Hall's remaining life energy, Marcus."

Darla whimpered. Sophie gasped in horror. Marcus simply stared at Gregory.

"I know." Gregory put up his hands to stay their protests. "It is an unsavory option all around, but you must also remember that there is a curse to worry about after the enemy rises. If the youngest Templeton controls the Serpent, that puts the battle squarely in *your* hands, *and* it prevents Connor from taking control of her. It also makes it so the battle happens on *your* schedule, not the enemy's. She is not known to make allowances for things such as family life." His eyes flashed with an old hatred.

Sophie shuddered. "It always comes back to this."

"How do you know it would work?" Marcus asked quietly. He studied Gregory suspiciously. "If I take control of that thing, how will it affect me? Will I lose myself? Will I become like her?"

"No." Gregory adamantly shook his head. "This is not a plot to make you a villain again, Marcus." He leaned close to the glass, his gaze serious. "This is a strategy to protect your life and the lives of everyone you love."

Heavy silence followed his words.

"You are a Defender, as well as the youngest Templeton," Gregory continued. "She cannot corrupt you or the other Defenders. Your goals and our enemy's are irreconcilable, hers to create chaos and destruction and yours to defend order and creation. Either you or she must win, and the surest way to victory is to direct her chaotic impulses to suit your goals. That was our original plan."

He glanced at Darla, who looked at him sadly. "We were going to control her so she could never hurt you because of the curse. Obviously, that failed." Gregory looked down at his hands with deep shame in his eyes. "You and the Defenders are now the last hope the world has at stopping her, and if you succeed, you will break the Templeton curse and redeem our family name."

Sophie glanced at Marcus, who returned her gaze uncertainly.

"No pressure or anything," Marcus quipped half-heartedly.

That got an amused grin out of Gregory.

"You are both extraordinary." He glanced at Sophie and Marcus with confidence radiating from his smile. "You have bested enemies far older and more powerful than you time and time again." His eyes twinkled as if he were savoring a joke. "With the six of you standing against this monster, I believe she will fall."

"Ten minutes." The guard poked his head in, then went back to his post outside the door.

The Templetons warily eyed the door.

"Um." Marcus fidgeted. "Thanks for the vote of confidence." He rubbed his arm, then glanced at Sophie. *Should I give them the invitation?* he asked in her mind.

Sophie smiled. *Go for it.*

Marcus took a deep breath. "There's something else, I guess." He pulled the invitation out of his jacket with shaking hands. Then he paused, uncertain.

Sophie stilled his shaking hands and took the invitation from him. There was no slot in the plexiglass to slip it through to the Templetons, so she slid her fingernail under the seal and pulled out the gilded card. She held it up to the glass with a smile.

"We wanted to invite you to our wedding," Sophie declared softly. She glanced at them.

Gregory's eyes widened as he read the scrolling script. He glanced questioningly at Marcus, who nodded in affirmation.

Darla's lip quivered, and she burst into tears.

"My darlings, what an honor," she blubbered. "We can't come, though, can we, Gregory? Not when we're stuck in this dratted place."

"On the contrary." Marcus finally got his voice back. "I worked it out with the EBI and the prison. You'll have a squadron of guards and elemental restraints, but they've agreed to let you come if you want."

"Oh, darling!" Darla threw her arms around Gregory's neck and sobbed.

Gregory held her tight, a half-smile curling his lips.

"Are you sure you want us there?" he asked incredulously. "After everything we've done?"

"Both our families need to witness our union," Marcus insisted. His eyes were at once sad and joyful as he watched his parents.

Gregory turned his face away and buried it in Darla's shoulder, then shook with silent tears.

Sophie took Marcus' hand.

When the Templetons parted a moment later, Gregory wiped his reddened eyes. He pressed a hand to the glass and smiled at them. "You honor us beyond what we deserve, but if you want us there, we won't miss it for anything."

"Absolutely." Darla nodded in agreement.

CHAPTER TEN

"The heat got turned up, didn't it?"

Charlotte fanned her and Sophie's faces as they stood behind Thicket Hall with the Defenders.

"Here you go, gals." Cedric's eyes glowed, and he swept his hand out to send a blast of cold air their way.

Sophie sighed in relief. "I'm glad it's summer, but you're right. This heat is pretty intense."

"It's got nothing on me," Liv quipped. Her hands were buried in the dirt, and she worked with Theresa and Janet, burning old plant matter to return the nutrients to the soil.

"Got that right, queen," Cedric affirmed.

"Anyone want some water?" Colin headed toward them with water bottles. As he handed them out, his eyes glowed.

Sophie took her bottle and saw rose-shaped ice cubes floating inside. She chuckled. "Thanks, Colin."

He saluted and continued handing out bottles. Her phone bipped, and she saw a text from her mother.

We'll pick up your dress in a couple of weeks. Also, do you need me to cover the deposit on the flowers?

Sophie tucked her water in the crook of her arm and frantically tapped back a response.

I left the check on my desk, I think. What do I owe for the dress?

She took a sip of her water, pleased to note it was already cold from Colin's ice. Her phone buzzed again.

I can't find it, sweetie. Are you sure you didn't take it with you? Don't worry about the dress. Your dad's paying for that.

Sophie's heart warmed. She dug through her pocket for her wallet, then heaved a frustrated sigh. The check she'd written that morning was still in her checkbook, signed and ready.

Sorry, Mom. I did take it with me. Can you cover it, and I'll reimburse you?

Sure thing, sweetie. Don't stress. It's all under control.

Sophie took a deep breath and tried to relax. There was too much going on at the moment for her to even begin to keep up with it all.

"Hey." Marcus' voice came from near her ear, and he

squeezed her shoulders. "You look peeved. Think we ought to break for food?"

Sophie put her phone away and leaned against him. "Maybe that would help. I'm overwhelmed."

He rubbed her arms comfortingly. "Relax, okay? I know it's difficult right now. We're getting married in a month and preparing for war at the same time. It's a lot."

"It's too late to move the date, isn't it?" Sophie snarked.

"A wee bit," Marcus chuckled. "Come on. Let's gather everyone up for milkshakes."

"Milkshakes?" Sophie perked up, and Marcus laughed.

The teens pulled up at Sonic in adjacent parking spaces and rolled down their windows. Sophie had carted Marcus, Janet, and Simon in her car while Cedric had chauffeured Olivia, Colin, and Theresa.

"Milkshakes all around," Cedric called to Sophie. "I'll cover them." He winked.

"That's real nice of you, bud. Taking care of us peasants," Marcus quipped.

"Hey, we *are* the king and queen," Cedric snarked back. He glanced at Olivia mischievously.

"Darn right we are," Olivia agreed with a grin.

"For free milkshakes, I'll gladly be a peasant in their kingdom," Simon stated, to everyone's amusement.

Two servers came out after they'd ordered, overloaded with greasy brown bags and drink cups. Most of them were dropped off at Cedric's car, and Janet stared through the window in alarm.

"Good *night*, Cedric! How much *do* you eat?" Janet exclaimed as he bit into his third burger. "Is there even a number on the amount of saturated fat in all this?"

"You don't want to know, Velma," Olivia quipped as she finished her mozzarella sticks. "I wish *I* could eat like that and never get fat."

"He's always been like that," Colin explained with an eye roll.

Sophie giggled as she dipped a fry into her milkshake. As she glanced at her friends, their smiles and silly banter created a warm feeling in her heart. Things were changing faster than she could process them, but right now, they could steal a moment to be kids again before the world ended.

The first Saturday in June was sweltering and humid, with tall cumulus clouds piling high in the sky far to the south. Sophie slathered on sunscreen and dressed in her swimsuit to go sunbathe with Millie, who'd urged her out to the pool as soon as breakfast was finished. Her phone buzzed on the counter, and she smiled as Marcus' name popped up.

You awake, princess?

Sophie snorted and picked up her phone.

Of course I'm awake. It's almost eleven.

She put the phone down and finished covering her face with sunscreen. Then the doorbell rang.

"Soph, will you get that?" her father called from the garage. "Your mom's at the store, and Mills is in the pool."

Sophie sighed and made her way to the door. The doorbell rang again, and she opened it a crack, not wanting to show some stranger her bathing suit.

A familiar grinning face greeted her. Marcus' arms were full of super soakers, and he was wearing a t-shirt and swim trunks.

"Marcus?" Sophie laughed. "I thought you had a party planned today."

"I did." He flashed her a smirk. "I let your dad know. He didn't tell you?"

"No." Sophie shot a playful glare at the garage. She opened the door and let Marcus in, and he gave her an approving once-over.

"Good. You're already dressed for the occasion."

Sophie blushed and shoved his arm playfully. "What is this, an early birthday party?"

"Something like that. You know, since we'll be busy that day." He winked and led her to the back patio. "Come on, babe. We got partying to do."

Sophie shook her head in disbelief. "You guys planned a surprise party for me?"

"We totally did!" Millie called from the pool. She grabbed one of Marcus' super soakers and filled it with water. "Mom's at the store getting cake and ice cream."

Sophie's heart swelled with love. "Aw. You guys."

Marcus kissed her cheek. "You're not gonna lift a finger today. Unless it's to have a super soaker battle, of course."

He stepped under the shade of the patio table umbrella and pulled off his shirt, revealing the well-developed muscles in his back and shoulders.

Sophie's face flushed, and her mouth dropped open. She hadn't realized how much Marcus worked out until this moment.

He turned to face her, saw her blush, and wiggled his eyebrows. "You like?" He flexed his biceps for good measure. "Haven't seen my progress for a while, huh?"

Sophie laughed nervously. "Uh. Yeah. Um." She squealed as Millie pegged her with a blast of cold water. "Mills!"

"You looked like you needed to cool off," Millie explained with a sly expression as Marcus cackled.

"You're in for it now, sis! Give me one of those super soakers!" Sophie ran toward the pool with a laugh. Marcus joined her, and soon they were circling the pool, trying to tag Millie as she bobbed around the various floats.

She cackled. "You'll never take me alive!"

"Wanna bet?" Marcus and Sophie cornered her, but Millie grabbed a float and held it up as a shield. Then she managed to hit Marcus square in the chest with a blast from her super soaker.

"Not fair!" Marcus laughed. "You have a whole pool full of water and shields."

"Tactical advantage," Millie corrected with a smug smile.

"Oh, really?" Marcus jumped into the pool, and Millie squealed with laughter as she tried to swim away.

Sophie jumped in and joined the chase, which somehow turned into Millie chasing Marcus instead. He scrabbled up the side of the pool and took off toward the forest with a teasing laugh.

"Get back here!" Millie shot after him with her super soaker, and Sophie chased his platinum blond hair, stepping on twigs and new grass in her bare wet feet. She didn't care. Running with her feet close to the earth, blossoming with life in the midst of spring, filled a deep place in her heart that longed for carefree days like this.

She lost sight of Marcus near the edge of the trees and slowed to catch her breath. "Marcus! Where'd you go—"

A wet hand clamped over her mouth, and strong arms wrapped around her waist and pulled her behind a tree.

"Shh!" Marcus whispered near her ear, quivering with laughter. He took his hand off her mouth and pushed into her mind with his. *I'm gonna jump out and chase her back.*

Sophie grinned. *I guess it's required. You're gonna be her big brother in, like, a month.*

Darn right. He wrapped his arms around her and kissed her cheek. Sophie thrilled at the sensation of his damp, warm skin against hers. *Plus, if we hide, I get to hold you close to me.*

Sophie blushed. *Marcus, you're playing with fire,* she warned teasingly.

Oh, am I? He turned her face and pressed a lingering kiss to her lips.

Sophie closed her eyes and leaned against his shoulder with a sigh.

"If you're gonna hide, don't make it so obvious. Oh, ew!"

They both turned to see Millie making a face at them and laughed.

"Get back to the pool, you gross lovebirds," Millie scolded.

Marcus took Sophie's hand with a sheepish look. "Shall we?"

"We'd better," she teased, arching her eyebrow at him.

The day passed in a beautiful blur of summer fun, barbecued meat on the grill, and cake and ice cream to celebrate Sophie's birthday early.

"We're coming up on the last four weeks before the wedding, and those are always the busiest," Joyce declared as they sat around a bonfire with marshmallows. "I didn't think we'd get another opportunity to celebrate, and besides, you needed a break, sweetie." She tucked Sophie's damp hair behind her ear and smiled. "You'll only be seventeen for a little while longer, and you deserve to enjoy being a teenager as long as you can."

"Thanks, Mom." Sophie smiled affectionately at her mother and bit into her toasted marshmallow.

"It's been kind of a rough introduction to adulthood for you," Marcus added. "If I've learned anything over the past year of endless overtime, it's that you have to make time to let loose and have fun, regardless of what's going on. If we lose sight of why we do all the hard stuff, we'll lose our fire for getting it done."

"Yep," Walter agreed succinctly. He chomped on his s'more and breathed a deep sigh of contentment.

"It's getting real," Sophie remarked. "Just yesterday, the venue called to get our final deposit. The *final* one. It's *nonrefundable.* That means we have to do this." She looked up when Millie started laughing and saw Marcus bent over double, shaking with silent laughter.

"What is so funny?" Sophie demanded.

Marcus straightened, wiping tears from his eyes. "Oh, man. *It's nonrefundable*, she says as if it's the apocalypse or something."

Walter chuckled, too. "Hey. It's a lot of money."

"It's true, but it's *just* money," Marcus countered. "You know, if something happened, no one would be mad at us for moving the date or losing a few hundred dollars on a deposit." He put a sunburned arm around Sophie's shoulders.

She arched an eyebrow. "Says Mr. Money Expert with his compound interest. You know how much a few hundred dollars would grow to become in ten years?"

Marcus laughed again, then fixed her with an earnest but joyful gaze. "I can't wait to spend my life with you. Don't ever change, Soph." He kissed her forehead.

Caught off-guard, she stared at him as her heart melted.

"Ew!" Millie scoffed. "Quit being so mushy."

"Tell me about it," Walter quipped as Joyce laughed.

CHAPTER ELEVEN

June passed as days of sweltering, busy overtime at the school and even busier nights as Sophie prepared for her wedding. With Thicket Hall to keep alive, venues to confirm, last-minute details to decide, and the occasional service cancelation to navigate, Sophie felt like she didn't have time to savor her last weeks as a single lady.

The day before her eighteenth birthday arrived before she had time to process where the time had gone. She was glad her family and Marcus had thought to celebrate earlier in June. Her schedule was booked until after the wedding, and then she'd be off to Gatlinburg with Marcus for a week away from it all.

Though she was excited, under all the stress, her heart clenched with apprehension at the thought of leaving Thicket Hall for as long as a week.

"Girl, you deserve it, and you *need* it," Charlotte insisted as she helped Sophie change into a beautiful navy-blue dress for the rehearsal dinner. Once they were both dressed, she took Sophie's arm and walked with her toward the door of Nurse Bonnie's office. "You can't keep working yourself to death. You gotta recharge. Besides, we can hold down the fort just fine."

"Charlie's right," Nurse Bonnie agreed. She shooed Sophie and Charlotte toward the door. "You girls go enjoy this rehearsal dinner. You've both been working yourselves to the bone." She patted their cheeks, then kissed Sophie's. "You're gonna make a beautiful bride, sweetie."

"Thanks." Sophie pulled Nurse Bonnie into a hug, then gave Charlotte a meaningful smile. "Both of you."

"That's what I'm here for, girl," Charlotte affirmed. "Gotta make sure you don't keel over before you make it down the aisle."

Sophie chuckled and followed Charlotte to her car. She'd agreed to the tradition of traveling separately from the groom the night before the wedding, mostly for old-fashioned fun for anyone who managed to catch them together. She caught sight of Marcus heading for his car as they passed Thicket Hall. He snuck a glance in her direction, gave her a heart-melting wink, and blew her a kiss.

Sophie grinned stupidly back and blew a kiss back.

"Y'all better not be making eyes at each other, fool," Charlotte scolded loudly, to Marcus' amusement.

"That goes for you too, Miss Angel," Peter agreed. He stepped into Sophie's line of vision, blocking Marcus from view, and gave her a teasing glare as she laughed.

Sophie handed Charlotte her keys and slipped into the passenger seat. Janet, Olivia, Bri, and Leslie piled into the backseat, squirming and squealing as they tried to get comfortable.

Sophie glanced back with a chuckle. "Don't kill each other. I need all of you for tomorrow."

"That's it. I'm not being a pancake anymore." Olivia wiggled up, then flopped into Bri's lap and draped her long legs over Janet's and Leslie's laps. "From now on, you guys are my seat."

"Not sure that's entirely up to state law, Liv," Janet noted, trying to shove Olivia's legs off.

"For real," Leslie agreed. She eyed Olivia's stilettos with apprehension.

"Can it, Velma, unless you want me in *your* lap," Olivia retorted.

"Just drive, Char," called Bri past a mouthful of snack cake.

Sophie laughed and let their shenanigans soothe her heart. Charlotte turned on their favorite music, and they jammed as they drove to the Brown Hotel, a historic, opulent hotel in downtown Louisville. The beautiful lights on the façade of the hotel entrance twinkled merrily as they got out and headed inside.

"Oh, wow." Sophie turned in a circle as she stepped into the grand ballroom they'd decided on for the ceremony. Tears rose in her eyes. The square platform on which she'd be married tomorrow had been covered with gorgeous navy-blue fabric, and towering over it was an indigo arch decorated with yellow and white flowers that looked like stars peeking out of the night sky. The navy-blue fabric trailed off the platform and created an aisle down the length of the room, flanked by dozens of chairs covered in silver or gold fabric to denote their families.

"Girl, this is gorgeous!" Janet squealed. "If Simon and I hadn't decided on a waterfall theme, I'd totally do this."

"It's way more beautiful than I imagined," Sophie murmured.

"Not bad." Olivia surveyed the room with an appreciative gaze. "Not the theme I would have picked, but whoever decorated it did a great job with it. I'm convinced."

Sophie laughed. "It means a lot to have your approval, Liv."

"Come here." Olivia strolled over to Sophie and fussed over her hair. "I can't let you go through rehearsal looking like this."

"Didn't have much time to get ready." Sophie chuckled. After Olivia finished, she inspected her newly curled hair with a smile. "You always do a great job. Glad you're doing my hair tomorrow."

"Well, I wasn't gonna let anybody else do it. They'd screw it up!" Olivia scoffed.

"Bro!" Peter's awed voice echoed through the room as the guys came in. "This is *insane*! Oh, I'm totally stealing this idea when I get married."

"About time you guys showed up," Bri teased.

Sophie jumped as arms wrapped around her from behind.

"What do you think, princess?" Marcus murmured near her ear.

Sophie chuckled and relaxed into his embrace. "It's amazing. It's getting real fast."

"I know."

"Hey!" Peter scolded them. "Don't get too cozy."

"What, I can't hug my almost-wife at our rehearsal?" Marcus retorted.

Peter narrowed his gaze. "As long as you don't sneak off, I guess it's fine." He winked at Sophie, who blushed, then laughed. "Just teasing."

The rehearsal passed in a giddy haze of nerves and apprehension. Everyone had to practice walking in and in what order, but the officiator kept it fun and upbeat.

As Walter took Sophie's arm and practiced walking her in, Sophie smiled at him. "You doing okay, Dad?"

"Don't ask me stupid questions like that, Sophie Bear," Walter replied. His voice trembled. He was on the verge of tears.

Sophie laughed and hugged his arm. "I love you, Dad."

"You're trying to make me blubber like an idiot, aren't you?" Walter said gruffly as he wiped his eyes.

"Of course not," Sophie teased. "Why would I want to do that?"

"You're a wench." Walter chuckled. "A rotten wench." They paused at the foot of the platform.

"Now, Walter, you'll lift the veil, and Peter, you'll come escort her to Marcus," announced the officiator.

Walter tucked Sophie's hair behind her ear and kissed her forehead.

Sophie smiled at her dad, and her lips trembled.

"Dang it, Soph, if you cry right now…" Walter laughed, and as he blinked, a tear ran down his cheek. "It's just the rehearsal. Oh, heavens, how am I gonna get through this?"

Sophie hugged him, and Walter gripped her tightly, shaking with tears.

Charlotte and the bridesmaids sniffled as they watched, and the groomsmen exchanged meaningful glances. Pete, waiting for Sophie at the edge of the platform, looked on with a smile, his green eyes shimmering. Sophie glanced at Marcus, who'd covered his mouth with his hand, tears glistening on his face.

"Get it all out now," Joyce scolded as she stepped up beside Sophie.

Walter grabbed for her, still sobbing, and Joyce wrapped him in a bear hug with a tender laugh. "Come on, big guy. We can do this."

Sophie laughed and patted her dad's back. "Love you."

"Love you too, Sophie Bear," he replied from Joyce's shoulder.

The rest of the rehearsal went smoothly. Walter even flashed Sophie a thumbs-up from his seat in the front row with Joyce, who kept a comforting arm around his waist. Sophie and Marcus practiced their vows with giggles and mess-ups, and then they headed to the adjacent ballroom for their rehearsal dinner.

Sophie ate her fill and then some, exhausted by nerves and her shift at work. As she sipped chamomile tea and began to slow down, she felt Marcus' eyes on her and glanced over.

His psionic presence pushed faintly against hers as if he

were trying to whisper. *The stars are out. Want to head outside for a couple of minutes?*

Sophie smiled a little. *Sure,* mon cher. *How do you suggest we sneak past Char and Pete?*

He smirked. *Head to the bathroom. I'll do a bait-and-switch with Simon.*

Sophie furtively glanced down the table at Simon, who gave her a subtle grin, then turned back to his meal.

You guys. She gave Marcus a teasing smile. *Naughty, naughty.*

Marcus winked.

Sophie excused herself to head to the bathroom, and Simon got up to get Janet more coffee. As she paused near the bathrooms, she heard a boyish yell from the doorway of the ballroom.

"Marcus!" Simon shouted. "Come kill this thing!"

"Simon, you big scaredy cat!" Janet cackled. "What is it, a spider or something?"

"No, a wasp!" Simon was convincing, his voice high as if he were terrified. "Pretty big one. It flew around here." He pointed at the bathrooms.

"On it, bro," Marcus replied. Sophie saw him hurry across the ballroom, and she slipped out to the courtyard to wait, then hid behind a tall oak and peeked up through the branches to admire the stars.

A moment later, she heard quiet footsteps in the grass. *Princess?*

She stifled a giggle. *Behind the oak.*

Marcus rounded the tree with a grin. *It worked beautifully.*

Simon's a good actor. She chuckled.

Marcus pulled her into his arms and held her close for a long, quiet moment.

It's our last night as just Sophie and Marcus, he noted. *Tomorrow, we'll be the Jenkinses.*

Sophie blushed and buried her face in his chest. *I know. It's crazy and romantic and so not logical, but it makes my heart happy in ways I can't even explain.*

Marcus lifted her chin and gazed earnestly into her eyes. *There wasn't going to be a perfect time for our lives to start, babe. Personally, I feel much stronger knowing that when we walk into this battle, we'll be one in every possible way.*

Sophie smiled bashfully. *You're right. It's just a lot to take in.*

"Where are they?" Peter's teasing growl echoed through the courtyard. "I'm gonna kill me a groom if he doesn't quit running off."

"I know *that's* right," Charlotte agreed. "Ooh, Miss Bride ain't getting none of my underdone brownies at this rate!"

Marcus and Sophie glanced at each other in amusement, then huddled behind the tree. Marcus cupped her face in his hands and kissed her gently. *I love you. I can't wait to marry you tomorrow.*

Sophie hugged him and kissed his cheek. *Ditto. I love you too. So much.*

"Hey!" Peter rounded the tree with a roar of laughter and playfully tackled Marcus. "You sneaky little devil! Caught you red-handed."

"Oh, no! Not this! Anything but this!" Marcus reached for Sophie dramatically as Peter dragged him away, but his eyes danced with laughter. "I love you, Sophie!"

Sophie giggled as Peter rolled his eyes. "Love you too,

mon cher!" Sophie blew him a kiss, then squealed as Charlotte snatched her arm and dragged her back to the door. "Char! I love him!" She made a show of reaching for Marcus' hand. "Don't separate us like this! Oh, cruel fate!"

That got a chuckle out of both boys.

"Quit all that foolishness and get your hind end in here," Charlotte scolded past hoots of laughter.

CHAPTER TWELVE

It was finally here. The day Marcus had dreamed about, stressed over, and fought for with all his strength. He'd barely slept last night as his thoughts had gone wild with anticipation and worry.

Yet he couldn't stifle his shaking hands as he adjusted his tie in front of the mirror. He wished it was over, and he was whisking Sophie away to Gatlinburg for their well-deserved honeymoon. He also thrilled at the knowledge that the best was yet to come.

There was a knock on the door, and Marcus glanced back as his dad Robert stepped inside. His dark eyes twinkled with unshed tears.

"Looking mighty fine, son."

Marcus smiled warmly at their reflections as Robert stepped up behind him and clapped a hand on his shoulder.

"Thanks, Dad."

"It's awful hot, though." Robert fanned his face. "Summer weddings. Sheesh."

Marcus laughed. "There's ice water downstairs."

"I know, I know." Robert's smile faded. "Listen. I wanted to tell you something."

"Okay." Marcus turned to face him, ready to listen to whatever words of wisdom—or good old-fashioned Robert-Jenkins-style scolding—he was about to receive.

"I just talked to, um, your mother and father." Robert tripped over the words, and he glanced at the floor as he spoke.

Marcus' heart fell and leapt in a single instant. "I see." Their presence would cause quite a stir. Bound with permanent elemental restraints or not, the Templetons were not welcome in most elemental circles, not after everything that had happened over the last four years.

"They talked to me a few minutes ago." Robert rubbed his cheek absentmindedly. "Thanked me and your mama for taking such good care of you and raising you. I told 'em it was mostly Denise. They said she must have been a fine woman for you to come out as such an exceptional young person." Robert wiped his eyes and gave Marcus a watery smile. "I couldn't agree more."

Marcus' mouth fell open, and his wary heart warmed at the thought of the Templetons praising his mom.

"Darla even kissed my cheek." Robert furrowed his brows and shook his head with a laugh. "That took me by surprise."

Marcus stifled a laugh. "Wow. That's...really something, Dad."

"Anyway." Robert blushed and cleared his throat. "They're waiting. They said they'd like to come in and see you, but only if you approve."

Marcus' mouth went dry. "They want to see me?"

"Are your ears working, son?" Robert playfully tugged Marcus' earlobe.

Marcus laughed and swatted Robert's hand away. "Yes, Dad." His smile fell away. "I'm just surprised that, um, you're okay with it." He glanced dubiously into Robert's eyes.

Robert gave a short nod, then grasped Marcus' shoulders. "You don't ever have to feel any guilt about letting more people who love you into your life. I don't care who they are. I only care that they love you. There's good in them, and it's stronger every time I hear about them. Maybe because some exceptional young man and his almost wife worked their magic on 'em." Robert pulled Marcus into a hug. "I'll always love you, son."

"Ditto, Dad." Marcus' eyes watered as he hugged Robert. Then his dad smiled and headed for the door, and Marcus' heart began to pound again.

A moment later, two familiar figures appeared in the doorway, flanked by armored guards.

Darla, in a charcoal-gray dress and red heels, took one look at Marcus and clapped her hands over her mouth.

"Oh, darling, look," she whispered to Gregory.

Gregory stared at Marcus. His platinum-blond hair was pulled back neatly, and he was wearing a beautiful black suit. He gave a polite nod. The pair stopped a few feet from Marcus and waited.

Marcus gazed at them, unsure of what to say or do. He wrung his hands and produced a wobbly smile.

"Uh. Hello."

"Hello, darling." Darla bounced on the balls of her feet,

clearly itching to scoop Marcus in a hug. He realized he'd inherited the nervous habit from her.

"Hello." Gregory's smile broadened as he took in Marcus' tuxedo and slicked-back hair. "You look incredible."

"Thank you." Marcus rubbed his hands down the front of his jacket, then dropped his polite smile and sighed. "I, uh. I heard what you guys said to my dad. I wanted to say thanks."

"Oh, of course, darling," Darla gushed. "We meant every word." She opened her mouth to speak again, but Gregory put a gentle hand out, and she closed her mouth, her eyes flashing with impatience.

Marcus glanced at them, wariness and warmth battling for dominance in his heart. He'd said what he felt, and he could tell both were reining themselves in, waiting for his permission to speak again. That put the ball in his court. This was how they'd been since Thicket Hall was spiked.

"Well, uh." Marcus started bouncing on his feet and stopped himself. "I'm glad you guys could come."

Gregory's amber eyes crinkled, and Marcus thought he saw moisture shining in them. "Receiving your invitation was one of the happiest moments of our lives. Thank you for letting us be here."

Darla nodded her agreement, then dug into her purse for a tissue.

"You are exceptional, Marcus," Gregory whispered. "I have no doubt that you and your new bride will enjoy a lifetime of happiness, and I wish nothing more for you than that." He glanced at Darla and gave her a tender smile, and she returned it.

Emotion welled in Marcus' throat. He could feel the sincerity radiating from both of them, welling through their magic and into their voices and eyes. Though residual mistrust and trauma kept him from bounding into their arms and embracing the parents he had not known existed, a glimmer of sunlight found its way through the walls he'd built.

He stepped forward and glanced at Gregory's hand, then reached out.

Gregory's mouth fell open, then he reached back, and Marcus grasped his hand and squeezed in a friendly handshake. He looked into Gregory's amber eyes and smiled.

"Thank you," he told him, and tears choked his words. "Not just for coming here today. For saving Sophie's life. For saving mine from the…" Marcus' voice trailed off, and he gave a nervous laugh. "Well, you know."

Gregory released a heavy sigh. He gripped Marcus' hand with a radiant smile, then nodded as his eyes filled with tears.

Darla sniffled, beaming at both men as she patted her cheeks dry with a tissue.

Marcus turned to her next, and her gray eyes, the mirrors of his, shone with joy. He took her hands and squeezed them. "Thank you. You gave me up so I would have a chance to live. I couldn't have asked for more than that."

Darla burst into sobs, though to her immense credit, she refrained from throwing her arms around Marcus. "Darling boy!" She rubbed her thumbs over the backs of his hands. "I'm happier than I've ever been, seeing you like this, so happy and strong." She looked deep into his eyes and smiled. "You've made us both so proud. You deserve this day to be perfectly happy."

Marcus dipped his head in acknowledgment, then glanced at them both and let go of Darla's hands. "I hope you'll enjoy the day, despite…you know." He glanced at the guards beside them, but Gregory stepped forward and gently lifted his chin.

"Nothing could stop us from being here." Gregory's amber eyes flashed with a familiar glint of determination.

Marcus smiled, then nodded.

"There *is* something we need to tell you," Gregory put in hesitantly.

Marcus' smile faded. "Okay. What is it?"

The Templetons glanced warily at each other.

"Well, you see, darling," Darla put in, "Gregory's trial is next month." She glanced at her husband.

Gregory took a steadying breath. "It will be decided what I'll be charged with among the thousands of counts the prosecution has drawn up," he continued. "All sentencing options have been put on the table, and…" His voice trailed off, and his gaze dropped to the floor. "I will put up no defense."

Marcus' breath caught. He stared at Gregory, speechless, and his chaotic thoughts ground to a standstill.

They had *thousands* of potential charges, and Gregory wasn't going to say a word in his own defense?

"Do you have a lawyer?" Marcus asked quietly.

Gregory shook his head. "No need," he whispered. "There is more than enough evidence. Why run from the truth?"

Darla squeezed Gregory's hand, sad but resigned.

"What about Trevor?" Marcus pressed. He cleared his throat to rid it of the lump building there. "Isn't there anything he can do?"

Gregory shook his head again and put up a hand as if to stop Marcus from saying anything more.

"It was my request," Gregory explained and met Marcus' gaze. "While I appreciate your willingness to forgive and even to try to lessen my guilt, I cannot go on as I have, always dodging justice and refusing responsibility." He lifted his chin and gulped, but his eyes were firm as he gazed at Marcus. "It is high time I accept the truth."

Marcus bit the inside of his lip as tears welled in his eyes. His heart broke and healed in the same instant as he stared at the man he'd once been intent on killing. The man who'd brought him into existence and somehow won his respect just as Marcus began a new life. Now Gregory had most likely ended his own by being silent in his criminal trial.

Marcus blinked. Tears escaped despite his best efforts.

Gregory studied him sadly, then gingerly reached out to put a hand on his shoulder.

Marcus' walls of mistrust and shame crumbled, and he pulled Gregory into a tight hug. His sobs broke loose as he clung to his father.

"Oh, darlings," Darla murmured, her voice trembling with tears.

Gregory made a soft noise of surprise, but he held Marcus and wept with him.

"I'll be at your trial," Marcus declared. "Sophie and I will both be there. Even if you won't defend yourself, we'll be there to speak for you. I don't know what good it'll do, but I'm not about to let you walk through hell alone."

"Dear boy," Gregory replied. He held Marcus at arm's length, his teary eyes radiant with joy. "No matter the outcome, I am whole again because of you."

Marcus smiled and nodded. His heart was calmer, as if it had finally found something it had lost. He glanced at Darla, who dabbed at her wet cheeks with a tissue. Then he pulled her into a hug, too.

As expected, Darla clung to him and freely wept on his shoulder. When she pulled back, her makeup was a mess.

Marcus chuckled. "You might want to fix that."

Darla laughed. "Oh, darling, don't worry. I'll look flawless again before the ceremony." She patted his cheek with a smile full of motherly affection.

There was a knock on the door.

The Templetons glanced at it warily, then returned their gazes to Marcus.

"We won't keep you from your preparations any longer," Gregory stated. He took Darla's hand, and they turned toward the door.

Darla paused and glanced back. "We both love you with all our hearts, Marcus."

Gregory nodded, and they studied him with looks of worried expectation as if waiting for his response.

Marcus' throat went dry. He'd just begun to return their affection. He had no idea how to respond to that or if he was even ready to reciprocate their love.

He opened his mouth, then shut it again and gulped. Then he nodded with a tender smile. It was the most he could do for now.

Gregory nodded in understanding while Darla's lip trembled. She gave half an affectionate smile, and in tandem, they turned and left the room.

Peter came in as they left and stared after them in shock.

"Bro. What the actual—"

"It's cool," Marcus reassured him. "They came in to give me their good wishes."

"They were invited?" Peter scratched his head. "Bold of them to come."

"I'm glad they're here," Marcus replied firmly, his eyes still on the door.

Peter gazed at him with an arched eyebrow, but his expression softened when Marcus looked at him.

"All right, man." Peter put his hands out. "It's your wedding day, and they're your folks. Whatever makes you happy."

CHAPTER THIRTEEN

Sophie headed down the hall, carrying the front of her massive wedding gown in a bundle so she could walk without tripping over it.

"Girl, I still think they didn't hem it right," Charlotte muttered past an armful of Sophie's train.

"Hopefully, someone in the bridal party brought a sewing kit," Sophie replied. They were on the hunt for a needle and thread to sew a button that had fallen off the back of Sophie's dress.

"It's all clear," Janet noted as she scouted ahead. She waved them around a corner. "No groom in sight."

"We gotta hurry," Bri stated as she checked her watch, clicking behind Sophie in a pair of navy high heels. "Forty-five minutes until showtime, and I still got your eyeshadow to do!"

Sophie rolled her eyes. "It'll be fine. It's just a button. Worst case scenario, we safety pin it."

"Do you know how tight this bodice is?" Olivia snarked. She walked on the other side of Sophie, carrying the second half of the train. "Everyone will see it if you pin it. The button *has* to be fixed."

"Aye aye, Liv." Sophie chuckled. "You're the fashion expert, not me."

"Darn right," Liv snarked, then gasped and stopped dead.

Sophie stopped, too. "What's wrong?"

"Look." Olivia pointed down the long corridor, and Sophie saw a flash of platinum-blond hair.

"Oh, no. Is it Marcus?"

"Worse," Janet squeaked.

Sophie took a closer look at the approaching figures, flanked by guards, then gaped.

The Templetons *had* come.

Her heart twisted with twenty different emotions.

"Just a little farther, guys." Janet beckoned to them, keeping her gaze on the Templetons as they drew nearer.

Sophie kept her gaze on the floor though she watched the Templetons from her peripheral vision. As they reached the door of the bridal party's room, the Templetons paused a few feet away.

"Hello, Miss Briggs." Gregory's silky voice was almost sheepish.

Sophie, along with Charlotte, Olivia, Janet, and Bri, looked at him warily.

Gregory, handsome in a pitch-black suit, had Darla on his arm. She'd curled her beautiful blonde hair and wore red heels and lipstick to contrast with her dark-gray dress. At least she hadn't worn white to upstage the bride, Sophie thought.

Gregory stepped forward and clasped Sophie's hand, then lifted it to his lips and kissed it.

"I'd hoped we'd be able to give our good wishes before the ceremony," Gregory told her with a genuine smile.

"Darling girl, you look radiant," Darla commented as she stepped up beside her husband. Her smile was forced, but her eyes were kind.

"Thank you," Sophie replied, then realized she was holding up the bulk of her dress and likely looked odd. "We're just on our way to get a small repair done." She nodded toward the door with a nervous chuckle.

"We won't keep you," Gregory began, but Darla stepped toward Sophie.

"What happened?" she asked.

"Just a button," Charlotte explained, holding up the pearlescent button that had fallen off.

Darla's eyebrows took on a determined slant, surprisingly reminiscent of Marcus' expressions.

"Hold on, darling. This won't take long." She handed her purse to Gregory, then rifled through it and pulled out a small sewing kit.

"No way," Charlotte muttered under her breath.

Darla clicked over to Sophie, then paused. "If you don't want me to help, please say so," she murmured quietly. "I'll understand."

"It's all right," Sophie replied. She glanced at her awestruck friends, then at Darla, then lifted her curled hair over her shoulder. "We didn't know if we'd be able to find anyone who could sew. It was serendipitous to run into you."

Darla blinked in surprise, then gave a small smile. "I'm a

fashionista. I've learned to make my own clothes over the years. Buttons are child's play." She took the button from Charlotte, and Sophie felt a vague, tickling sensation as Darla sewed it back on.

"Uh-oh." Janet glanced back down the hall in the direction they'd come. "I see some of the groomsmen. We'll have to hurry this up and get Sophie hidden."

"Just need to tie it off." Darla's voice was muffled by the needle she held between her teeth. She tugged the threads, then fitted the button through the loop and patted between Sophie's shoulder blades. "There you are. Good as new." She glanced back, and her eyes widened. "Oh, dear, you'd better get going. Here comes Marcus." Her voice reflected her affection when she said Marcus' name.

Darla ushered Sophie and the girls into the bridal party's room, then turned to leave.

Sophie clasped her hand and smiled. "Thank you. Not just for fixing my button, but for being here for Marcus." She glanced past Darla at Gregory, who smiled in acknowledgment. "Thanks for saving my life at least twice."

Gregory's mouth turned up in a familiar lopsided grin. "It was the least I could do. You are exactly the right person for our son, and I knew it the moment the two of you stood together the first time. I wish both of you all the happiness in the world."

Sophie nodded and smiled, her heart welling with warmth. "Thank you."

Darla patted Sophie's cheek. "You make Marcus happy, and you stayed by his side throughout all the difficulties of the past few years. That's all I could ask of my darling son's bride-to-be."

Sophie blinked in surprise, then gave them a watery smile. "I'm glad you came. Without you, I would have never met the love of my life, so thank you."

Darla stepped out and took Gregory's hand, and they smiled tenderly at one another. Then they both dipped their heads to Sophie and disappeared down the hallway.

"Sophie, if you could only see your fool right now," Charlotte squealed. She had Sophie and Marcus positioned on either side of a wall, unable to see each other, but both in the frame for Charlotte's photos. "He ain't never looked so fly."

Sophie heard Marcus chuckle. "I can always count on Charlotte to pump me up."

"Just you wait until you see your girl." Charlotte joined their hands around the doorframe, snapped a few more pictures, and squealed again. "Oh, these are such good pictures. You're gonna love them. Now tell her you love her, fool."

Sophie felt Marcus squeeze her hand, then felt the ripples of his psionic presence in her mind.

I love you. So much. You don't even know how much.

Sure I do, Sophie replied with a shy smile. *You're about to marry me. You must love me a lot.*

"Keep it up, boy." Charlotte's camera snapped as Sophie smiled.

I can't wait to see you, Marcus told her, his mental voice wistful.

Ditto, mon cher. Just don't cry, okay?

Marcus laughed aloud. *I can't make any promises.*

"These make cute pictures, but not being able to hear what's causing all these reactions is making my skin crawl," Charlotte remarked.

I barely slept last night, Sophie admitted. *I was so nervous, thinking about everything that could go wrong. Now that we're here, I feel like it's a dream come true.*

Marcus' emotions welled with warmth and joy. *I feel the same, princess.*

"Oh, that's it," Charlotte encouraged. She snapped a few more pictures, then grinned in triumph. "All right. Sorry, fool, but it's about that time."

Sophie's breath hitched. "Already?"

Marcus chuckled. "You've been dying to get married, and now it's too soon?"

"No, of course not," Sophie clarified with a laugh. "It just seems like the morning has flown by."

Marcus squeezed her hand once more, then reluctantly let go. "I'll see you very soon, princess. I love you."

"I love you, too." Sophie could barely speak past the happy tears in her throat. "I can't wait to marry you."

"Ditto." She heard the emotion in Marcus' voice and wiped a stray tear from her cheek.

"Y'all gonna make me ruin my makeup," Charlotte complained as she patted under her eyes with a tissue. "Get outta here, fool. Come on, girl. Let's get you ready."

Twenty minutes later, Sophie clutched her father's arm in front of the inner chapel's doors. The bridal party gathered in front of them, and occasionally, Charlotte glanced at Sophie and gave her a thumbs-up. Marcus was already inside, safely out of view from where Sophie and her father stood waiting.

"You can't look at me, and you can't talk to me while we're walking down this aisle," Walter instructed, resolutely looking forward.

"Why, Dad?" Sophie asked with a chuckle.

"You know exactly why," Walter retorted. Moisture shimmered in his eyes.

"We'll never get this moment back," Sophie pleaded. The music started, a gorgeous ballad Sophie and Marcus had picked out together, and her heart raced. "All right. Here we go."

Janet and Simon, the first in the procession alongside Millie, the flower girl, waved at Sophie and gave encouraging smiles. Sophie smiled back and waved them on as the chapel's doors opened.

Olivia and Cedric went next, Olivia strutting on custom stilettos dyed to match the bridesmaids' colors. She blew a kiss to Sophie as she passed by, and the bride chuckled.

Then came Bri and Luke, and Leslie and Vince, all nodding and waving to Sophie.

Last were Charlotte and Peter.

"You got this, girl," Charlotte whispered. Peter gave Sophie one of his crinkling emerald smiles and a thumbs-up.

"You're an angel, Soph," he told her. His eyes welled with moisture. "Marcus is gonna flip his lid."

Sophie laughed. "Thanks, Pete."

After they disappeared inside and the doors closed behind them, Sophie took a deep breath. Joyce walked up behind her and squeezed her, then kissed Walter's cheek.

"You're up, my loves," she whispered.

"Let's go, kiddo." Walter's voice was thick with emotion. He lowered Sophie's veil over her face, and she hugged him.

"I love you, Dad."

Walter hugged her back, his shoulders shaking. "Doggone it, Sophie Bear. I told you not to talk to me."

Sophie laughed as Walter kissed her cheek.

"I love you too, kiddo. So much."

They positioned themselves in front of the chapel door. Then the door opened, and a navy carpet with white rose petals sprinkled along it stretched out before them. The guests stood, and Sophie noticed the Templetons near the back. Darla clasped her hands and gaped admiringly at Sophie, and Gregory smiled as she passed.

Appreciative murmurs and sighs went up from the crowd as Sophie made her way to the front. She snuck a glance at Marcus, and her lips trembled. He looked dashing in his black tuxedo. His white vest sparkled with gold stars, and his long blond hair was tied back like a Victorian gentleman's.

He'd clamped his hands over his mouth, his eyes wide and watering as he stared at her. It was oddly reminiscent of Darla's reaction. She *was* his mother, Sophie thought. Peter, who was standing next to him, whispered something in his ear. He shoved a tissue into Marcus' hand, then turned back to the front and clasped his hands in front of him.

They paused at the end of the aisle, and Sophie turned to her father to let him lift the veil from her face.

Walter kissed Sophie's forehead, as he had at the rehearsal dinner, but he held it together, to his immense credit.

Sophie grinned and kissed his cheek. Then she took Peter's arm and let him lead her to her place beside Marcus.

"I had to talk your guy down from the all-out ugly-cry ledge," Peter whispered as they walked.

Sophie stifled a laugh. "That doesn't surprise me."

Peter gave her a little bow as he offered Sophie to Marcus, and Sophie smiled at him.

Marcus let out a shaky breath as he took Sophie's hand and led her to the front.

"You look. I can't even," he stuttered.

Sophie beamed at him. "Ditto, *mon cher.*"

The ceremony began, and to Sophie's relief, it was short and sweet. She recited her vows with all the sincerity and love in her heart, then slipped Marcus' silver band onto his ring finger, admiring the engraved crescent moons circling the band.

Marcus' eyes shone as he recited his vows. His fingers trembled as he placed her ring next to her engagement ring, a gold band with a sun pattern engraved on it.

The officiator joined their hands and glanced at them, and Sophie held her breath as he uttered the words that would seal the deal.

"I now pronounce you husband and wife."

The guests erupted into raucous applause, and Marcus grasped Sophie's hands, disbelief and joy crowding his emotions.

"We did it," he whispered.

Sophie nodded and beamed as fireworks went off in her tummy and elation surged through her in bursts of golden joy. "We're officially married."

"Kiss her!" the groomsmen shouted, and the guests laughed.

Marcus glanced at Sophie, and though he tried to keep it casual with a shrug of his shoulders, his eyes glimmered with deep affection.

"Guess we should give them what they want," he teased.

Sophie didn't wait. She went up on her tiptoes and threw her arms around his neck, then kissed him firmly. He sighed with deep contentment and kissed her back, and the guests clapped and cheered.

After they'd taken all the pictures Charlotte demanded, Sophie and Marcus made their way to the reception. Sophie clung to Marcus' arm as fatigue overtook her.

"You look like you could use some coffee." Marcus chuckled as he wrapped his arm around her waist.

Sophie sighed. "That would be lovely." They stepped under the decorative arch that led into the banquet hall, and cheers erupted. Cameras flashed, and they paused under the arch for the obligatory picture. Then Marcus led her to the head table and pulled out her chair, which was decorated with a banner that had a golden sun stitched on it.

"Have a seat, my lady," Marcus murmured near her ear as he pushed her chair in. "I'll find some coffee for you."

"Thanks, babe." Sophie tiredly propped her chin on her hands, watching him go with a blissful smile.

"Well, it's done, girl!" Charlotte hurried over and plopped next to her, then set a plate full of food in front of her. "You are officially a married woman."

"Yeah." Sophie was still watching Marcus, her eyes lingering on the contrast of his blond hair against his suit.

Charlotte laughed and shook her head. "You ain't looked at him like that since the first day he walked you to the greenhouse, you know that?"

"I just can't believe we're married," Sophie replied dreamily. "He's all mine."

"Girl, he ain't had eyes for no one else since that combat class when you fought each other." Charlotte nudged her, giving a tearful smile. "Precious. Now, eat up before you disappear."

Sophie reluctantly turned her attention to her food and nibbled a chicken tender. Marcus returned after a moment with a steaming mug of coffee.

"All they had was French vanilla creamer," he told her apologetically. He took the seat next to her, which was decorated with a crescent moon.

"It's all good." Sophie took several gulps of the coffee and sighed in relief.

"You gonna inhale that if you're not careful," Charlotte scolded. "Leave some room for cake, too."

"This is why I needed you, Char," Sophie noted. "I'm going to have to be led by the hand from this point on."

"If somebody had slept last night, they wouldn't be in this mess." Charlotte arched an eyebrow, but her expression softened when Sophie pouted. "All right, girl. You know I got you."

The celebration passed in a blissful haze. Sophie and Marcus cut the cake, and Sophie laughed and put up her hands as a shield when Marcus tried to smash a piece into her face. Then came the dances: Sophie and Marcus first, then the father-daughter dance. Sophie tried not to cry as Walter hugged her but ended up bawling on his shoulder while he bawled on hers. Everyone laughed and wiped their eyes as the music ended.

"Love you, Sophie Bear." Walter kissed the top of her head.

"Love you too, Dad."

Then it was time for the bouquet toss. Sophie stood with her back to the women and giggled as she heard them chattering.

"I'm so gonna catch it," she heard Liv say. "I don't care if I have to knock someone out."

"Liv!" Janet scolded. "You wouldn't do that!"

"Bet," Liv retorted.

Sophie shook her head, then let the bouquet fly and turned around. She clamped her hands over her mouth and laughed as the girls scrambled for it. Liv *did* catch it, nearly tripping over a table to snatch it as it flew close to the ceiling.

"I got it!" she shouted, then shot a sly grin at Cedric. He smiled nervously back.

"What about the garter toss?" Peter asked. He glanced at Marcus and wiggled his eyebrows, and Sophie blushed.

"Peter!" she scolded.

"I don't even know if Sophie is wearing one," Marcus retorted matter-of-factly, "and if she were, I certainly wouldn't retrieve it in front of all of you." He flicked a glance at Sophie, his eyes glittering with amusement as he noted her blush.

"Very classy, son," Walter shouted over the chaos. "Father of the bride approves." He gave Marcus a thumbs-up as everyone laughed, and Marcus returned the thumbs-up with a grin.

"However," Marcus went on, "I do have a garter that I can toss." He slipped a thin band of lace out of his pocket and motioned at the guys to gather, then winked at Sophie.

Sophie gratefully smiled back. She hadn't cared for the tradition when it was suggested by her wilder friends, but Marcus had a way of strategizing. She wouldn't have to show her stocking-covered legs, and they could still let the guys get in on their version of the bouquet toss.

He sent the circlet of lace flying, and the guys nearly trampled each other trying to get it. Reggie rose to the top of the pile, his bright smile making Sophie laugh hysterically.

"Lookie what I got, doll!" He shouted to Charlotte as the girls crowded around her with teasing shouts and whoops.

Sophie wrapped her arm around Charlotte's shoulders and grinned at her best friend's blush. "Well, well. We gonna have another wedding soon, Char?"

"Shut up, Sophie." Charlotte playfully shoved the bride's arm. "Go snuggle your man or something. Dang."

"Snuggling would be nice." Marcus' voice sounded near Sophie's ear as he wrapped his arms around her shoulders.

Sophie grasped his hands. "Yeah, it would."

"Y'all can do that on the honeymoon," Peter snarked. "Where are y'all going, anyway?"

"Gatlinburg," Sophie replied.

"Classic," Simon put in as he passed with Janet on his arm. "Great place. That's where I proposed." He exchanged affectionate looks with Janet.

"We also didn't want to be too far away in case anything happened with Thicket Hall," Sophie continued.

"Yeah," Marcus agreed. Some of the joy had left his words. Sophie cupped his face between her hands.

"We're still gonna have a great time," she told him firmly.

He smiled back. "That we are, princess."

"As you should," Janet confirmed with a nod. "The two of you deserve some time off, especially now that you're married."

"Speaking of time," Charlotte put in, hurrying over as she looked at her watch. "If y'all want to make it to East Tennessee by sundown, you'd better start heading that way."

"Already?" Marcus glanced around. "I feel like we just got here."

"It's been a few hours, actually," Janet affirmed. She

grinned at them. "Don't worry. We will help you make a clean getaway."

Sophie went with Charlotte and her bridesmaids to the changing rooms, and they helped her get into regular clothes.

She packed her wedding shoes in her duffle bag, then eyed her humongous dress.

"Don't worry about your dress," Janet soothed. "We'll take care of it and get it to your house for you. I mean to your and Marcus' house." Janet corrected with a nervous laugh as Sophie blushed. "Just take yourself and your luggage. We'll help you get out to the RV."

"Thanks, guys." Sophie pulled her bridal party into a group hug. "I couldn't have done this without you."

"Well, of course not," Olivia snarked, though she ruffled Sophie's hair affectionately. "You two have a safe trip and have lots and lots of fun." She winked and patted Sophie's cheek.

CHAPTER FOURTEEN

The girls piled Sophie's luggage into the back of the Briggs family's RV. Sophie noted with amusement that the guys had tagged the RV with chalk paint, featuring the phrases Just Married and Honk for the Newlyweds across the back.

Sophie and Marcus stood before their friends, who all hugged the new couple.

"You guys have fun, okay?" Janet smiled. "We'll hold down the fort. Don't worry."

"We got this. Right, guys?" Simon glanced at Olivia and Cedric with a nod.

Sophie grinned. "I trust everyone."

"We mean it," Charlotte scolded. "Don't worry about a thing. Thicket Hall will be fine without you for a week."

Sophie and Marcus exchanged glances, and though Sophie could see the worry lingering in Marcus' eyes, his joy and excitement outweighed it.

"They're right," he told her. "This time is for us to enjoy. Let's make the most of it."

Olivia, Bri, and Peter snorted. Sophie sighed and rolled

her eyes, and Marcus arched an eyebrow. "Seriously? That wasn't an innuendo."

They burst into guffaws. Olivia and Bri clung to each other, and Peter wiped his eyes.

"It's too dang fun to tease you." Peter sighed. "Now, *git*. You got more important things to do than stand around talking to us." He winked at Marcus.

"All right, guys. See you when we get back." Marcus leapt up the RV's steps, then held out a hand for Sophie, eyes twinkling.

"Bye, everyone! Thank you so much for everything." Sophie blew her friends a kiss, and they waved and cheered as she stepped into the RV and shut the door behind her.

Marcus gave a happy sigh, and his shoulders slumped. "We made it to the getaway."

Sophie chuckled. "You've been waiting all day to get away, haven't you?"

"Sort of," Marcus admitted sheepishly. "All this peopling gets to you when you're an introvert at heart." He stepped close and took her hand, then led her to the front of the RV. "It's just you and me for the next week."

"Yeah." Sophie sighed, then glanced at their glistening new rings. "It'll be amazing."

"Definitely." Marcus kissed Sophie gently, then settled into the driver's seat. Sophie took the passenger seat, then tapped her dad's GPS, which was set up and ready to direct them to Gatlinburg.

"Aw, Daddy." Sophie smiled. "He took the time to get everything ready for us."

"He's a great man," Marcus put in with a smile. He

buckled his seat belt, then started the engine. "Ready to go, wifey?" His smile morphed into a smirk.

Sophie melted into blissful laughter. "Definitely, babe."

They made one stop to get strong gas station coffee before they set out in the fading light for Gatlinburg. Marcus was determined to make it to the campground before true nightfall, which would be around 9:30. Having left close to four, it was doable, but given the way Sophie kept swaying in her seat from exhaustion, she wasn't sure she'd be able to help keep Marcus awake.

They paused at a rest stop for a thirty-minute nap. Sophie slept in the back while Marcus dozed in the driver's chair, convinced that if he laid down, he'd sleep for hours. Then they were off again, with enough gas station snacks to feed an army.

Sophie didn't care. She'd made it through the most blissful, stressful day of her life, and they were going to celebrate with their favorite junk foods and tons of music played through the RV's ancient speakers.

The food, music, and amiable chatter kept them awake long enough to pull into the campground as the sun set behind the Smoky Mountains a few hours later.

"Sophie Jenkins," Marcus murmured as he parked the RV.

Her heart melted. It was the first time she'd heard her new name—her married name—out loud. She glanced at him with a bashful smile.

His brow was furrowed as if he were unsure. "Sophie Jenkins. Hmm." He grinned, his eyes alight with joy. "I like."

"I do, too," Sophie replied shyly.

"We share everything now, princess. A last name, a home, two cats, our life." Marcus shook his head, blinking back tears. "It's sort of hitting me now. Sorry." He wiped his eyes.

Sophie's lips trembled. "I know. It doesn't seem real, but it is."

"This is one time in my life that my reality is way better than any daydream." He unbuckled his seat belt, then crossed to her seat and helped her up.

She gazed into his happy, tearful eyes and felt the intense joy running rampant in his magic. Her heart swelled until it could burst. She twined one of her hands through his and reached up with the other to touch his cheek.

"Ditto," she whispered.

They spent the next half-hour connecting the water and electricity so they'd have utilities, with Marcus' phone playing music from his back pocket. Sophie hummed along as she took care of the familiar process and stole glances at the darkening sky.

"It might be fun to sit on the roof and stargaze," she mused.

"I like that idea," Marcus agreed with a contented sigh. "First, though, I need a shower."

"That's a good idea." Sophie secured the water connection, then headed inside and grabbed her pajamas from her luggage. Marcus mirrored her, and as they walked toward the bathroom, Sophie abruptly stopped. Marcus did, too, and they looked away from each other with nervous laughs.

"Whoops." She laughed. "Wasn't thinking. Who's gonna go first?"

"After you, princess. I can wait." Marcus opened the door for her and gestured inside. "Just don't use up all the hot water," he teased.

Sophie laughed. "Married just a few hours, and we're already arguing over the hot water?"

"Not an argument. Just a suggestion." Marcus smirked.

Sophie's heart melted again. With a sudden rush of boldness, she stretched up on tiptoe and kissed him.

Marcus' hands found her waist and pulled her close. Then he kissed her with a calm, joyful intensity, once, then twice, then three times.

Sophie gave a squeak of surprise. She'd only meant to kiss him once, but now that they were here, she didn't want to let go.

Another thought occurred to her, making her face flush with heat.

She didn't *have* to let go, and neither did he.

Marcus pulled back. "Sorry," he murmured, his voice rough with passion. "I, uh, got a little carried away."

Sophie stared at him, heart racing, face burning, mind swirling with confusion. Why was he apologizing? Why were her hands trembling on his chest?

Why did she suddenly want to run away and hide?

"I-I'm gonna go shower," she stuttered.

Marcus let her go, shaking himself from the spell. "Yeah, yeah. You go ahead."

Once inside, she clutched the edges of the sink and tried to calm her racing heart. Reality was sinking in, and though it was exhilarating, it was also terrifying.

She was *married* to Marcus now. All their previous boundaries were null and void, and they belonged fully to each other, as they'd promised at the fountain.

How long would it be before they decided to take the next logical step in their relationship? What would have happened had their surprise kiss continued? Had Marcus' habitual gentlemanly restraint not stopped him?

The answer shouldn't have terrified her. They were married now. Even so, her hands shook.

Sophie noticed her bright red ears and cheeks and splashed cool water from the sink onto her face. She dug makeup remover out of her toiletries and scrubbed until the layers of foundation, bronzer, highlighter, lipstick, and who knew what else were off, and all that was left was her lightly freckled face, rubbed raw by the cleansing.

A soft knock on the door made her squeak and jump.

"Yes?" she called shrilly.

"Just wondering," Marcus called, his voice muffled by the door. "How long are you gonna be? I'm pretty tired. Don't want to fall asleep while I'm waiting." He chuckled.

Sophie let out a breath of relief, then frowned with guilt. She wanted to feel excited. She'd been waiting anxiously, just like Marcus, for the day when they'd be able to do away with boundaries altogether.

If they were both tired, though, there was a chance this question could wait, giving her time to calm her nerves and come to terms with their new life together. She also wanted to jump right in, as much as the thought made her blush. She didn't want to keep Marcus waiting, after he'd been so patient for so long.

"I-I'll be quick, I promise," she called back to him.

"No rush, babe. Take your time." His words seemed to imply something beyond taking a shower, and even through the door that separated them, she could feel his emotions swirling to a calmer state, deepening with understanding.

Sophie let out another relieved sigh. She pressed her hands to the door and leaned her head against it. "Thanks. I love you."

"Love you too, princess."

Once she'd bathed and dressed in her pajamas, her nerves were significantly calmer, and the exhaustion from the day set in. She swayed on her feet in front of the mirror as she brushed her teeth, then traipsed out and headed straight for the bed.

"No stargazing tonight?" Marcus asked as he paused in the bathroom doorway. "I was looking forward to that."

"So tired," Sophie mumbled in response. She collapsed face-down on the mattress as Marcus laughed.

"We got all week," he remarked and gave her a tender smile. "I'm pretty beat, too. Might not be a bad idea to go straight to bed. See you in a bit." He disappeared inside the bathroom, and Sophie closed her eyes and almost fell instantly asleep. The soothing sounds of the shower water faded to nothing.

The next thing she felt was movement, then gentle arms around her shoulders and waist. She opened one groggy eye and glanced into Marcus' eyes, then realized he was holding her.

"You were taking up the whole bed, princess," he whispered, his eyes crinkled in amusement.

"Sorry," Sophie mumbled.

Marcus chuckled and laid her down with a soft pillow under her head, then switched off the lamp on the tiny nightstand next to her. Sophie settled in, then stiffened as she felt movement beside her.

Right. They were married, which also meant they shared a bed. Yet another change that seemed enchanting and terrifying at the same time.

Sophie's eyes widened, and she held her breath as Marcus wrapped his arms around her and pulled her close, then covered them both with the blanket and let out a happy sigh.

"I've been waiting to cuddle you like this for years," he murmured near her ear.

Sophie's heart melted even as her ears burned. "Yeah," she managed to squeak in reply.

He huffed a laugh through his nose and pressed against her back. "I distinctly remember a certain princess telling me she couldn't wait to marry me so she could snuggle me anytime she wanted," he pointed out. "Yet she's all flustered now that it's here."

Sophie couldn't speak past the butterflies crowding her chest. She'd daydreamed about what this moment would feel like, but nothing had prepared her for the shockwaves of joy, desire, and sheer terror she felt with him so close to her.

Still, her eyes drooped with exhaustion, and she let out a reluctant yawn.

Marcus laughed. "It's okay. I get it. We're both tired *and* irresistible." He kissed her cheek, then ran his fingers soothingly through her hair. "Trust me when I say there's absolutely no rush. We can get used to our new life together one small step at a time. No pressure. No worries."

Sophie let out a relieved sigh. "You understand me so well."

"Always." Marcus kissed her cheek again, then settled down on the pillow behind her. "Goodnight, princess. We'll feel better in the morning. I love you."

"Love you, too, babe." Sophie relaxed into his embrace and let his warmth and the soft rhythm of his breathing lull her back to sleep.

Marcus woke with the first morning birdsongs outside the window. He drew in a deep breath and moved to stretch, but something—someone—grasped at him and grumbled sleepily.

He froze in mid-stretch and glanced down, blinking the grit from his eyes as he tried to piece together what was going on.

Sophie's dark hair and familiar features came into focus, and Marcus grinned groggily as it came back to him.

They were married, and this morning was the dawn of the first day of the rest of their lives.

Sophie shifted, and her messy hair tumbled over her face. Marcus gently brushed her hair back and wrapped his arms around her. She snuggled close, her magic sluggish and gray in her half-awake state. The colors swirled to a standstill again as she fell back into a deeper sleep.

"Look at her," Marcus whispered to himself, repeating a line from one of his favorite movies. "I would die for her. I would *kill* for her. Either way, what bliss."

Sophie remained asleep, her fingers curled loosely around his pajama shirt, and Marcus sighed contentedly and closed his eyes to drift off again.

A moment later, he startled out of a half-asleep daze as the sound of distant howling echoed through the air. It wasn't loud enough to wake Sophie, but Marcus came wide awake.

Had those zombie creatures followed them here? Were they in danger?

He glanced at Sophie's peaceful form. Determination and adrenaline pumped through his veins as he carefully untangled her fingers from his shirt and tucked the blankets around her.

He was going to protect what he loved.

Sophie woke as a shiver rolled through her. She pulled the blankets tighter around her shoulders and turned onto her back, then stretched out her hand to find Marcus.

All that greeted her touch was the residual warmth from his presence.

Sophie blinked herself fully awake and tilted her head up. She didn't hear the shower running or the sounds of cooking. In fact, the RV seemed unnaturally silent.

"Marcus?" she called. No answer.

That was weird. She would have thought he'd be eager to greet her on their first morning together.

She sat up and rubbed her arms, which had goosebumps. Shivers crawled down her neck and spine, and she grabbed the throw blanket from the end of the bed and wrapped it around her shoulders as she clambered out of bed. A quick check of the bathroom confirmed that Marcus wasn't in the RV.

Maybe there had been a problem with the water. Sophie slipped on her flip-flops and hurried to the door. As she opened it, her teeth chattered. She'd expected some chill in the early morning air, but it was mid-July. It shouldn't have felt like an early spring morning.

Gritting her teeth against the cold, she stepped down and checked around the RV, but Marcus wasn't there. She eyed the security station at the entrance to the RV park and was about to start walking when the chill abruptly intensified.

She glanced behind her as her intuition and psionic ability went haywire, sending signal after signal that she couldn't interpret. Her hackles rose as she studied the apparently empty tree line of the forest beyond their RV. What on earth could be out here?

The answer hit her like a lead weight. What if one of the Serpent's servants had followed them here? What if she intended to hurt them while they were separated from Thicket Hall and the other Defenders?

Sophie headed for the RV's door. She had to get dressed and hunt down whatever this was. If the Serpent's servants had Marcus and she had to fight for him, she'd need every advantage she could get.

As she touched the handle of the door, she paused. A shadowy, shapeless silhouette congealed near the trees.

Sophie called her life magic, holding it at the ready near her side, and took her hand off the door. If this was a pure death elemental creature, she could take it easily.

The shadow took on a familiar form, and she noted bright silver lines marking a crown around its brow and cuffs around its wrists and ankles.

She squinted. "Marcus?"

Glowing eyes locked on her.

"What are you doing?" she asked.

The silhouette took a few steps closer, and the chill became nearly unbearable. Sophie tugged the blanket tighter around her shoulders and warily eyed Marcus' shadowy form.

"Geez. No wonder the others don't like being around you when you're like this."

His silver eyes crinkled in laughter. Then he held out his hand.

Sophie gulped. She'd felt an insane chemistry with Marcus in his elemental form, but that was when she was the Greek goddess Persephone come to life. She didn't know what would happen if she touched him now.

Still, she trusted him with all her heart. She stepped toward him, shivering like mad, and took his hand.

Their linked hands provided the channel of communication they'd been lacking. Sophie still shivered, but now she could see images and feel emotions.

Marcus seemed amused. He showed her a picture of herself, radiant with flowers in her hair and around her waist with a golden halo of life magic.

"You want me to change, too?" she asked.

Marcus nodded.

Sophie smiled. It would make being around him much more pleasant, but she still needed to know something.

"Why are you in your Defender form? Did something happen?"

Marcus shook his head. A memory played in Sophie's mind, and seeing herself through his eyes, with her goofy sleeping face and hair all messy, made her blush with embarrassment. Then a distant echo of a sound, a wolf howl, and Marcus tucking her in and heading out to investigate.

"Did you find anything?" Sophie asked.

An image of a regular wolf yelping and running away from Marcus' death elemental form made Sophie chuckle.

"Poor thing. You scared it half to death."

A surge of irritation washed over Sophie.

"I know, I know. You were protecting me." She glanced up and smiled.

His eyes crinkled again. Then he let go of her hand and gave a little bow as if to encourage her to transform.

Sophie giggled. "All right, all right. Fine." She glanced at the other RVs parked nearby. "Maybe we ought to go farther out, though, so we don't freak out the other travelers."

Marcus nodded, grabbed her hand, and led her into the trees.

When they were in a clearing, Sophie closed her eyes and repeated her mantra. The sunlight on her skin felt heavenly, juxtaposed with the chill of Marcus' presence. As she completed her transformation, joy surged through her veins, and she turned in a circle and laughed.

"I always forget how awesome this form is," she noted, her voice tinkling and merry.

You look incredible. Marcus' voice echoed in her head, loud and thundering.

Sophie gasped. "You can talk now?"

Marcus stepped toward her, and now she could see his facial features, lit by her golden glow. He smirked, looking irritatingly handsome, and Sophie melted.

I've been practicing, he replied in her mind. *I still can't talk out loud, but I can do this. It helps.*

It really does, Sophie agreed. *It makes you seem more human and less ghostly.*

Marcus chuckled. He took her hands, then lifted one to his lips and kissed it.

Sophie's breath caught. The insane chemistry of their Defender forms was back in full force, and being newlyweds added to it.

I love you the way you are, but being together like this makes my day, Marcus told her.

Ditto, Sophie replied. She gazed into his eyes and thrilled as he moved closer, stopping to rub his nose against hers as always. Then he moved in for a kiss.

Sophie put both hands against his ebony face and

stopped him. *How is your energy? I don't want you doing what Simon did.*

I'm okay, princess. Marcus put his hands over hers. His magic coursed with a desire that bordered on a need to be close to her warmth.

Sophie was breathless with anticipation.

His eyes never left hers. His hands moved up her arms, resting briefly on her shoulders before moving down to her waist. He pulled her against him and pressed his forehead to hers.

Sophie's confidence soared as their chemistry reached new heights. She let her arms drape over his shoulders, then tilted her head back and batted her eyelashes. To her satisfaction, Marcus' magic lit up with crimson desire.

Don't look at me like that, Marcus murmured in her mind.

Sophie didn't reply, just pressed her lips against his, letting the kiss linger much longer than she normally would. Then she kissed him again, noting that his cold arms pulled her tighter with each kiss.

She didn't know whether it was their Defender forms causing such intense desire or whether it was years of delayed gratification, but whatever the cause, she didn't want it to end.

She decided on one more kiss, and then they'd change back to their normal selves. She could feel Marcus' magic flagging as he sustained his Defender form.

She locked her gaze on his, then cupped his face in her hands and kissed him softly.

Sophie, he crooned in her mind, his psionic voice husky and dark. *You're playing with fire.*

Sophie grinned, but to her surprise, she didn't blush. Instead, she let go of her Defender form, and Marcus let go of his, and they stood holding each other, breathless and tense with desire.

Sophie felt shyer as she gazed into Marcus' smoldering eyes, though her desire hadn't abated. He reached up to trace her jaw with his fingers, and the crazy tingling she'd been so used to suppressing to protect their boundaries rose to the surface.

She'd been scared and tired the previous night, but curiosity and craving had taken over.

"Maybe…um." Marcus cleared his throat and blinked as dark red blossomed against his pale cheeks. "Maybe we should head back to the RV?" He gave her one of his lopsided grins, and his magic swirled crimson, violet, and gold. "I mean, we shouldn't leave it unlocked, you know." He cleared his throat again, but his mental presence gently brushed hers. *Are you still afraid? Are you sure you're ready?*

Sophie, buoyed by the otherworldly confidence she'd felt a moment ago, smirked at Marcus. She rested her hands against his chest, satisfied to see the crimson in his magic amplify at her touch.

I'm not afraid, she responded.

"Hmm. I think that's a good idea, *mon cher*," she said aloud. She let her fingers trail down his arms before grasping his hands. "It's chilly out here anyway." She moved closer to him, staring at his mouth. "Wouldn't it be nice to be somewhere safe, warm, and *alone?*" She pressed a lingering kiss on his cheek.

"Alone. Yeah." Marcus' voice was barely a whisper as he

brushed his nose against hers. Sophie saw his magic bursting with dark red passion.

Sophie leaned teasingly close but pulled back at the last second with a mischievous smirk. "Well, Hades, let's go." She took a few steps backward, giggling at the look of disappointment on Marcus' face. Then she ran toward the tree line.

"Hey! Wait up! That's not fair!" Marcus sprinted after her with a laugh.

Sophie glanced back as she reached the parking lot. He wasn't far behind, and his eyes held a competitive and determined glint.

"Get back here, Persephone!" he shouted.

She shrieked with laughter, then squealed as Marcus caught her around the waist and hefted her over his shoulder.

"Got you now," he teased breathlessly. He carried her up the RV's steps and set her on her feet, but his hands never left her waist.

She smiled. "Am I in trouble, Mr. Agent?"

"So much trouble." He pulled her close and tilted her head back. "I'm pretty sure it's against some code to be *this* irresistible." He traced her jaw with his thumb and smirked. "Gonna have to do something about that, Mrs. Jenkins."

Sophie blushed. "What do you suggest, *mon cher*?"

In answer, Marcus smirked, twined his fingers through hers, and led her down the hall.

CHAPTER FIFTEEN

The last morning of honeymoon bliss dawned cloudy and humid. Sophie gave a groggy yawn as she kicked the covers off, then laughed as Marcus pulled her against him.

"I don't want to go home," he complained against her back.

"I know, babe, but Thicket Hall needs us," Sophie reminded him. "Plus, Dad's expecting the RV back for Lake Cumberland next week."

"When did you become the adult of the two of us?" Marcus teased.

Sophie chuckled softly. "On my birthday, I guess." She wriggled out of Marcus' grasp, then rolled over and kissed him. "Come on. Let's get up. We gotta make tracks so we can unpack before work tomorrow."

They grudgingly got up and began their preparations for the day, showering, cooking breakfast, and packing their things for the five-hour trip home. As they disconnected the electricity and water lines, darker clouds rolled in, followed by a chilly breeze laden with the scent of rain.

"Summer storm," Marcus noted. "That'll be fun to drive through."

Sophie glanced up as a raindrop pelted her forehead. Her heart sank at the thought that the blissful week they'd just enjoyed was the calm before the real storm.

"Chin up, princess." Marcus stepped close, noted her frown, and kissed her gently. "We just had an amazing week, and we're gonna go back to the fight stronger than ever."

Sophie took some comfort in Marcus' earnest gaze and the strength of his hands on her shoulders. "Yeah," she agreed.

An hour later, they were on the road home, and their favorite music played from the speakers. Sophie kept stealing glances at her phone, expecting a call from her friends or family.

Her conscience plagued her. How could she just drive away for a week and abandon her guardian? How dare she enjoy the sights and relaxing ambiance of Gatlinburg when back home in Bardstown, her friends were fighting for Thicket Hall's life?

What if the old oak had lost even more leaves? What if it was on Death's doorstep?

How was Charlotte doing with Thicket Hall's golden acorn? Did she remember to water it and give it sun?

All the questions Sophie had suppressed in her exhausted, blissful daze throughout the week were loud and clear in her mind, and she bit her lip to keep the tears at bay.

Although her friends had ushered them out the door the night of their wedding and showered them with good wishes, she wrestled with the weight of the fight to come. A week away hadn't fixed the problem. It had just delayed the inevitable.

They pulled into the Briggs' driveway several hours later, and Sophie hugged and kissed her family as they hurried out to greet the newlyweds.

"How'd it go? Did Old Bertha treat you well?" Walter lovingly patted the RV's sides. "I don't see any dents or scratches, so that's good news." He winked at Marcus.

"It was great, Dad," Sophie chuckled. "Marcus handled it like a pro."

"So happy you're back, sissy!" Millie squeezed Sophie, then stepped aside so Joyce could hug her.

"I hope you had a great time, sweetie," Joyce told Sophie, then kissed her cheek. "We're happy to have you back in town."

The guys hauled their luggage out of the RV and into Marcus' car.

"We'll be back later tonight for dinner," Sophie remarked. "Gotta unpack and make sure everything's settled for work tomorrow."

"Back to the real world, hmm?" Joyce sighed with a knowing smile. "Don't work too hard. Despite what's going on, you two deserve to enjoy being newlyweds. Don't forget to take joy in the little things."

Sophie smiled half-heartedly. "Thanks, Mom." She hugged everyone again, then slipped into the passenger seat of Marcus' car and waved as they pulled out of the driveway.

"Ready to head home, princess?" Marcus asked tenderly.

"Home," Sophie repeated with wide eyes. She glanced back at her family's home, and a wave of bittersweet nostalgia washed over her. While she knew her parents would always welcome her and Marcus for visits and trips, that was no longer her primary home.

She smiled shyly at Marcus as her cheeks warmed. Her home was now with him in his tiny one-bedroom apartment in La Grange.

As they pulled up to the curb a bit later, Marcus hurried to open Sophie's door, then swept her into his arms and carried her through the small yard to the front door.

Sophie laughed and clung to his neck. "You couldn't resist, could you?"

"Nope." He set her down on the porch so he could dig his keys out and unlock the door. Then he picked her up again, wiggled his eyebrows, and carried her over the threshold. "Welcome home, Mrs. Jenkins."

As soon as they were inside, the two cats ran down the hall. Nate nearly barreled over Sophie's new yellow kitten, Joy.

"Careful, Nate," Marcus warned.

"Aw, you guys came to greet us!" Sophie clambered out

of Marcus' arms and knelt to gather both cats in her arms. "You didn't tear up the place, did you?"

Nate meowed innocently in answer, while Joy, still much smaller and fluffier than Nate, crawled up Sophie's shirt and settled near her collarbone with a tiny purr. "How could I be mad at that?" she crooned.

Marcus chuckled. "You're gonna spoil 'em rotten now that you're the mistress of the house," he noted. He headed over to the dining room table, where Joyce had gathered their mail from the week, and thumbed through the envelopes with a sigh. "Bills, bills, bills."

Sophie smiled grimly and joined him at the table, still holding Joy. "Money flying out the window."

"Thankfully, our bank account is golden after all that overtime before the wedding," Marcus remarked with an eye roll. "Still annoying, though." He picked out a couple of decorative envelopes. "Here's some happier mail. Looks like wedding cards."

"We can open those after we unpack," Sophie scolded playfully.

"Says the girl who's holding a kitten," Marcus teased.

"I can hold my cat all I want in my own house." Sophie stuck her tongue out at Marcus.

He smirked. "Is that how we play it? This is your house now, and I'm just the peasant who lives here?"

"You just said I'm the mistress of this house," Sophie retorted.

Marcus took a step closer, a wicked glint in his eye. Joy jumped down when Sophie giggled nervously and took a step back.

"Last time I checked, little mistress, I was the master

here, and the master gets to tickle people who challenge his authority," Marcus crooned.

"Oh, really?" Sophie tried to stop giggling, then shrieked with laughter and tried to dodge Marcus' hands.

He grabbed her around the waist and pushed her gently onto the couch, tickling her sides and underarms relentlessly.

Sophie's eyes leaked tears of mirth as she wheezed with laughter. "Not fair! Stop it!"

"What's the magic word?" Marcus demanded.

"I don't know!" Sophie managed between hoots of laughter. "Please? Uncle?"

"Wrong! Now you'll have to pay the price, my dear. A kiss." His eyes sparkled with mischief.

"Fine!" Sophie exclaimed. "Deal. One kiss."

Marcus' tickling slowed, then stopped, and he leaned over her and rubbed his nose against hers. "Or maybe more?"

Sophie melted into a puddle of bashfulness. She knew what that smoldering tone in his voice meant.

As he brushed his lips against hers, Sophie's phone rang, vibrating against the floor. It had fallen out of her pocket during Marcus' tickling spree.

She ignored it when Marcus kissed her again and wound her fingers into his long hair, pulling him closer.

As their kiss progressed, the ringing stopped. Then the doorbell rang.

Marcus pulled away, and they glanced at the door in annoyance.

"I guess we better get that," Marcus said breathlessly.

Then he let Sophie up and smirked at her. "We can continue this later."

Sophie giggled. She smoothed her clothes and answered the door with trembling hands.

Charlotte stood on the doorstep. "Hey, girl!" She took one look at Sophie's face and snorted. "Do I need to come back later?"

"N-no, of course not!" Sophie cleared her throat to get the huskiness out of her voice, then ushered Charlotte inside. "How's it going?"

"I hate to interrupt y'all's newlywed bliss, but something's up with baby Thicket Hall," Charlotte declared as she sat on the couch between Marcus and Sophie. She pulled the acorn out of her pocket and held it out to Sophie. "It's not glowing anymore, and the outer shell is getting kinda dry and cracked-looking."

Sophie squeaked in alarm and took the acorn from Charlotte. She could still feel Thicket Hall's trademark rumbling hum, but it was distant and higher than normal.

"You've been watering it, right?" Sophie asked frantically. "No excessive sunlight?"

"Girl, you know I ain't gonna let that thing shrivel up and die," Charlotte teased. "I *am* capable of growing things, in case you forgot."

"No, of course not." Sophie sighed. She studied the acorn and pushed her psionic presence toward it, then grasped Charlotte's hand to let her into the conversation. *What's going on, big guy?*

Thicket Hall's rumble was weak as it replied. *Near the end I am, sapling. Acorn reflects what happens to tree.* Its hum warmed as it addressed Charlotte, who'd gone still. *Is still okay. No fear. Good job you did, taking care of me.* It turned its psionic energy toward Marcus next. *Will need to take my energy soon, I think. Better you do it than have enemy come on us when we are not ready.*

Charlotte gasped, and Sophie gave her an understanding look. She hadn't yet heard about Gregory Templeton's strategy to defeat the curse and put the Defenders in control of the Serpent.

Marcus studied the acorn with a scowl. *I don't want to have to do that yet. We still need time to gather our allies, the EBI agents from other states and friends and family.*

Go faster, saplings, Thicket Hall warned. Its hum was weak. *Time not on our side anymore.*

With that, its presence withdrew, leaving a lingering warmth in its wake.

Charlotte, Sophie, and Marcus exchanged wary glances, then stared at the acorn in Sophie's palm.

"I guess it's time to prepare for D-Day," Charlotte noted quietly.

Sophie sighed. "Yep. By the way, Char, no one else knows about the idea of Marcus taking what's left of Thicket Hall's life energy so he can control the you-know-what. It's not something we're totally set on yet. It was suggested by Gregory Templeton, and he's nothing if not a strategizer, but it's not our favorite idea." She glanced at Marcus, who nodded in agreement. "I'm sure you understand why."

Charlotte shivered. "I won't tell the others. Not until y'all make a decision about that, but the tree seems to think it's the best idea. Not like I want to see your boo kill our school again."

"Don't remind me," Sophie groaned.

Marcus scoffed. "Never thought I'd see the day when Thicket Hall would agree with Gregory Templeton of all people."

"Whatever the Defenders decide, I'll help," Charlotte affirmed. She looked earnestly at Sophie and Marcus, then rolled her eyes. "Even if your new hubs becomes a snake charmer."

Sophie managed a chuckle. "Thanks, Char. No matter what, we're better together." She locked arms with her best friend and her husband, and they smiled at her confidently.

"Darn right, we are," Marcus agreed.

CHAPTER SIXTEEN

Work at the EBI was in full swing on Monday. Marcus settled at his desk for the hour of office time he'd have before taking Sophie, Janet, and Simon down to the school for the day.

Dottie dropped in, left a cup of coffee on his desk, and ruffled his hair affectionately. "Good to have you back, Romeo," she teased. "Did the new Jenkinses have a good trip?"

"It was amazing," Marcus gushed. He glanced at a new photo on his desk, a Western-style sepia print they'd had taken in Gatlinburg. A velvet gown-clad Sophie had roped him for a kiss with a lasso, and he'd eagerly played the part of a smitten cowboy.

"That's a cute one," Dottie noted as she studied the picture. "You two have always been adorable together."

Marcus chuckled. "Thanks, Dottie."

"Oh, I wanted to leave something else." She pulled a file from the small stack of folders in her hand. "We might have a lead on Connor. Think you can look at this before you head out this morning?"

"Sure thing." Marcus' smile faded as he took the folder.

"Try not to worry," Dottie encouraged, patting his shoulder. "It'll all work out."

Marcus didn't reply as she left the room. He opened the file and scanned the contents. Blurred pictures from a security camera at a hotel showed a familiar burly figure with a ball cap and sunglasses and a screen shot confirmed the purchase of a plane ticket. The destination was Louisville International Airport. The date of arrival was too small to make out, but the month was a single-digit number.

Marcus' stomach sank. So, Connor was coming back for the final battle, giving them only a couple of months at most to prepare. Perhaps only weeks or even days. Chances were good that he'd been communicating with the Serpent, him being her chosen host, and had planned his arrival close to her preferred date.

This gave them a good indicator of when the final battle would take place and aligned with Thicket Hall's prognosis from Roscoe, Sophie, and the other life elementals who scanned it each day to monitor the progress of the spikes' disease. It also made Marcus' heart beat faster. He had to try to get Connor out of the way before that battle. If Connor got to the tree first and he took control rather than Marcus, their hope of winning the battle would almost certainly be lost.

Marcus grabbed the handset of the phone on his desk and paged Trevor.

"Jenkins, my main man. What's up?" Trevor's tone

remained boyish and carefree, although he was the interim Head of the EA.

"Just got intel about Connor's whereabouts. He's coming to Louisville sometime in the next couple of months. Maybe sooner. Give the order for Connor to be tracked down. We need him dead or alive at this point," Marcus declared. "If he gets to Thicket Hall before we have everything in place, we're done for."

"Understood. Will do." Trevor hung up as someone knocked on Marcus' door.

"Come in," Marcus called.

"Hey, babe." Sophie slipped inside, radiant as always. She grinned and patted her chest, where her silver name tag was proudly displayed. "Just got the new one."

Marcus' heart flipped. "Let's see it." He stood and examined her name tag. *Sophie Jenkins, Co-Lead Agent.*

"You like?" Sophie teased, her eyes glowing with affection.

"I love it," Marcus replied. He kissed her gently, but his smile faded as his gaze fell on the intel folder.

"What's wrong?" Sophie followed his line of vision and headed over to his desk. She picked up the folder and thumbed through it, her brown eyes hardening. "I see. Got a host to take down, huh?"

"Yep. Problem is, I can't read that arrival date. It could be tomorrow, or it could be September thirtieth." He flopped down on the sofa and sighed. "I've ordered agents after him. They're supposed to bring him back dead or alive, and if they bring him in alive, it might fall to me to ensure he doesn't get in our way. He's very slippery. He pulled that stunt with Simon's power last time, and if we've got him in our grasp…" His voice trailed off, and he rested his forehead in his hands. "We gotta make sure he's dead this time. For real." He glanced at her wearily. "There's too much at stake."

Sophie was silent as she put the folder back on his desk. Then she joined him on the sofa and curled up against his chest.

"I know it's not what you want, but if it comes down to it, I know you can do it," she told him sincerely.

Marcus scowled. His friends had encouraged him not to do it in the caves, but now he was kicking himself for not listening to his strategic mind. True, they'd thought the problem had taken care of itself when the machine blew up, but it was possible that he'd have to work up the courage to try again if Connor showed his face.

He thought about Gregory taking Caleb's life to protect them and shuddered. Connor had told Marcus he didn't have it in him to kill. Was he right? Was it ever worth taking a life, even to spare a loved one? Would he ever heal from it if he was forced into a situation like that?

"Why do I always have to be the bad guy?" Marcus muttered.

Sophie touched his face with a warm hand. "You're not the bad guy, Marcus. You never have been. The only thing that stops a bad guy with tremendous power is a *good* guy with tremendous power. *You* are that good guy."

She tapped his chest over his heart. "You protect what you love. Gregory did the same thing when he protected us from Caleb. It wasn't easy, and no one wants to have to do it, but if it comes down to it, *you can*. I know you can."

Marcus frowned as he gazed into her earnest eyes. He

knew deep in his soul that if her life was on the line, he'd kill in a heartbeat. Same went for any of his friends and the other Defenders.

In the heat of the moment, he'd take whatever action was necessary to make sure they all made it out alive. He'd nearly killed his own father when he'd thought Sophie had been taken from him. He had the potential. He'd almost killed before.

Admitting it sent shivers through him and twisted his heart into knots, though.

"When all this is said and done, and the you-know-what is gone for good, I'll never kill again," Marcus growled.

Sophie's pretty lips lifted in a smile. "When all this is said and done, you won't ever have to."

CHAPTER SEVENTEEN

For the next week, Sophie poured life energy into Thicket Hall. Charlotte, Professor Garver, and Nurse Bonnie stood behind her, lending her their strength and life magic as she pushed it into the sprawling root system of the behemoth tree.

She pulled back with an exhausted sigh and wiped her brow. "That'll keep it going for a few more days," she stated.

Is good, sapling. More time, it gives, Thicket Hall encouraged, its voice weak and the acorn's vibration dim in her pocket.

"At least we're not still dealing with that stomach bug. We can make progress on the tree instead of stopping everyone from losing their lunch," Nurse Bonnie noted.

Sophie's weary heart fell. "Yeah, but we're close to the end, so it doesn't matter. Why else do you think the sickness just disappeared?" She glanced bitterly at the edge of Bernheim forest, where she'd stood and cursed the Serpent's zombie creatures the day Princess' kitten had been killed. "They know it's only a matter of time. They don't care anymore."

Charlotte squeezed Sophie's arm comfortingly. "We know, girl. You can't say it's not helping, though."

"You're buying something we desperately need right now," Garver reminded Sophie. "You're buying time."

Sophie nodded. "Yeah. I guess so." She glanced at her watch as it chirped. "Oh, gosh. Janet's dress fitting." She slapped her forehead. "I almost forgot."

"Yeah!" Charlotte wrapped her arm around Sophie's shoulders. "We'll go get Ned's afterwards. Come on!"

"Enjoy the break," Garver called as Charlotte led Sophie toward the parking lot.

Sophie let her hair down and shook it out as they walked. The late summer heat had baked the top of her head for the last hour without Thicket Hall's foliage to protect it. All of its rust-red leaves had dropped to the ground, a monumental task for the groundskeepers to clean up. The tree's bare boughs and graying bark felt like a massive omen of death standing in the midst of Bernheim Forest's flourishing canopy of dark green leaves.

A memory of the skeletal silhouette of Thicket Hall against fire and the glow of a serpentine creature assaulted Sophie's mind—the memory she'd been forced to watch by the rock creature.

She gulped and shook her head to clear it. It wouldn't do any good to ruminate on the battle to come. They had to fight it regardless. There was no longer any stopping it.

"Try to smile, girl," Charlotte encouraged. Her voice was sad despite the smile she'd painted on for Sophie. "I know you're overwhelmed, but Janet needs us. She needs *you.*" Charlotte bumped her hip as they walked, then let Sophie into her car.

Sophie sighed and slipped into the passenger seat. "I know," she responded after Charlotte had gotten in and started the car. "I just feel hopeless right now, like we're charging into a battle we're doomed to lose."

"With that attitude, yeah, we're gonna lose," Charlotte noted matter-of-factly.

Sophie glowered at her. "Char. That's not helping."

"Neither is your attitude." Charlotte scoffed. "From where I sit, Miss Defender of Hope and Life, you're the one with the power to change your mindset. You have the power to change *everybody's* mindset."

"How can I do that when *I* don't have any hope?" Sophie shot back. "How can I be expected to prance around with flowers and joy when I'm *exhausted* to my bones and scared to death of what's gonna happen to everyone I love?"

Angry tears welled in her eyes. "I can't do this, Char." Deep resentment mingled with strangling fear and hopelessness formed a lump in her throat. "I'm sick of this. It's not fair. It's not *fair!* I just want it to be over!" She buried her face in her hands and sobbed.

Charlotte's hand rested on her back. "Get it out, girl. All of it. Right now."

Sophie leaned into Charlotte's quiet permission to grieve and rage. She pulled at her hair, shouted at the floorboard, and cried until she didn't have any breath left. By the time they'd pulled into the parking lot of the dress shop, Sophie felt she could gather her breath again. A free, empty place had opened in her soul as she unburdened it.

Sophie pulled in a shuddering, contented breath and

sat up in her seat as Charlotte parked the car. When she glanced at her best friend, she saw Charlotte's red eyes and wet eyelashes and knew she'd been crying with her.

"Bring it in, girl." Charlotte pulled Sophie into a hug.

"Thank you," Sophie whispered.

"I knew you needed to get it out," Charlotte remarked as she stroked Sophie's hair. "How long has it been since you let yourself cry?"

"Too long," Sophie admitted with a chuckle.

"You need to do the same for your boo," Charlotte told her as they separated. She fixed Sophie's hair and wiped the makeup off her cheeks. "He looks like a pot about to boil over."

Sophie nodded. "I'll talk to him soon. If we don't fall over from exhaustion first." She giggled. "Usually, we eat frozen dinners and watch TV until we fall asleep after work."

"That sounds super romantic, let me tell you," Charlotte joked. Sophie patted Charlotte's cheeks with a tissue, and the girls smiled at each other.

"Come on, girl. Let's go love on Janet," Charlotte encouraged.

A moment later, Sophie stood with Bri, Olivia, Leslie, and Charlotte and fluffed the end of Janet's beautiful train.

The bride-to-be stood with her hands pressed to her cheeks, trying not to cry as she examined her reflection.

"You look like a fairy queen," Sophie remarked. She

stepped over the platform Janet was standing on and fitted her tiara and veil to the top of her head.

"I can't even believe it," Janet squeaked. She sniffed and covered her mouth as her eyes watered. "I'm getting *married*."

Sophie squeezed Janet's shoulders and smiled affectionately at her. "You definitely are. It's gonna be wonderful. You won't believe you're married even *after* you're married. Trust me."

Janet giggled, then took Sophie's hands. "I'm glad we get to do this together, despite everything that's going on." She glanced at all the girls, her eyes pausing on Bri, her maid of honor, who stood with tears pouring down her cheeks and a snack cake in her mouth.

"Babe, I'm already crying," Bri scolded, her voice muffled by the food. "Don't get all poetic."

"Yeah, I don't want my makeup ruined today," Olivia put in. She blinked, trying to look indignant though her eyes were watering.

Sophie laughed with the rest of the girls, her tense heart warm and full for the moment. Then she touched Janet's cheek. "I know your wedding will be amazing, no matter what. I hope the battle will be won by the time you walk down that aisle with Simon and that you guys can marry in the middle of a perfect day full of sunshine. You deserve it."

Janet's lips trembled. Then she hugged Sophie, and Sophie hugged her back.

"Dang it, Soph," Bri sobbed. "I told you guys not to go there!" She ran up the steps and joined the hug, and the whole girl gang surrounded Sophie and Janet, laughing and crying and wiping makeup off each other's faces.

"We're either gonna have to buy stock in waterproof makeup or start being less weepy," Leslie noted with a laugh.

"Got you covered, Les," Olivia put in. "Hey, Velma, is it okay if I make an addition to your bridesmaid bags?"

"Whatever you say, Liv." Janet chuckled.

CHAPTER EIGHTEEN

The next two weeks crept slowly by. Sophie exhausted herself trying to keep Thicket Hall alive. Reinforcements from the regional EBI offices started to trickle in, expedited by Marcus' and Trevor's urgent pleas. Sophie, Marcus, and the rest of the Defenders had their friends and family on standby, and Headmistress Rogers had every faculty member on speed dial for D-Day.

The first Friday in August arrived, and with it, Gregory's trial date. Sophie and Marcus had requested the afternoon off so they could attend, and as Marcus somberly straightened his tie in the Jenkins' tiny bathroom, Sophie put a hand on his shoulder, then fussed with her hair and makeup. She couldn't seem to keep her thoughts focused on anything for more than a minute at a time. She was too worried about her new father-in-law and what his fate would be.

As she reached for her mascara, Marcus stilled her hand.

"It's gonna be rough," he muttered. "Don't know if I would go there."

Sophie pulled her hand back with a sigh. "As much as I hate to admit it, I think you're right." Her voice broke, and she avoided looking at her reflection.

Marcus hugged her, and Sophie cried on his shoulder. "I know," he soothed. He pulled back and held her at arm's length. "You sure you want to come with me? You don't have to. I totally understand."

"You're my husband, and he's my father-in-law," Sophie declared, wiping her cheeks. "How could I *not* be there?"

Marcus studied her tenderly, then nodded. "Not gonna lie. I don't want to go by myself." He blinked, and a tear ran down his cheek.

Sophie wiped it off and caressed his face. "You won't have to. I'm always here for you."

He took her hand and kissed it, and they exchanged meaningful looks. Then he led her out to the hallway and grabbed his keys from the table.

"No time like the present." He sighed.

The trip to the courthouse in Louisville where the trial was taking place passed in tense silence. Media vans surrounded the courthouse, and the parking lot was packed as they pulled in. Marcus' phone rang as he snagged a parking spot with his EBI permit.

"Dad?" Marcus answered. "You're here?" He glanced at Sophie, who smiled at him. At her urging, Robert had come to support his son. "Didn't expect that, but I'm glad. We'll meet you on the front steps." He hung up, then got out and walked Sophie to the front.

Robert met them on the bottom step and pulled Marcus into a long hug.

"Thanks for coming," Marcus began as he stepped away.

"I wouldn't have known the date and time if a little bird hadn't told me." Robert winked at Sophie and patted her shoulder, and she beamed at him.

Marcus gave Sophie a grateful smile, then took her arm and walked up the steps with Robert on his other side. As they went inside, Marcus flashed his EBI badge at the security officer, and Sophie did the same. They were let through without interference, but as soon as they reached the crowded marble hall of the courthouse, camera flashes and shouted questions assaulted them from all sides.

"Are you really Templetons' son?"

"Is it true Gregory Templeton almost killed you, Sophie?"

"Agent Marcus Jenkins and his new bride are here to witness the trial of the century. It's not just intrigue that brings them here. It's also family ties," declared a reporter as she tried to keep pace with them. "Tell me, Agent Jenkins, what's the outcome you're hoping for today?"

"Leave us alone!" Marcus shoved the reporter's microphone out of his face and broke into a run, tugging Sophie and Robert with him. "That way!" He pointed at a velvet-rope barrier in front of massive double doors. Security guards ushered them past the paparazzi and into the relative safety of the courtroom.

Sophie could still hear the media buzzing outside, but the courtroom was eerily silent. The prosecution waited at their gleaming oak table near the front, with two rows full of witnesses. The judge shuffled papers on his bench and quietly chatted with a secretary. The jury flipped through spiral-bound books full of what Sophie guessed were the charges against Gregory Templeton.

The defense's table was empty.

"Since you've volunteered to be defense witnesses, you can sit here," stated the security guard who walked them down the carpeted stairs to the front. He gestured at the row of seats directly behind the defense table. "Don't think anyone will call you, though."

Marcus exchanged dubious glances with Sophie. Then she shot him a hopeful smile.

"Come on." She tugged Marcus to their seats and gripped his hand as they sat down. Sophie noted a few of the prosecution witnesses staring and pointing at them, then whispering with their colleagues.

She ignored them and turned to face the front.

The chatter from the hall suddenly amplified in volume, and Robert sighed heavily.

"Think they're here," he noted gruffly.

Marcus' face went pale.

A moment later, the courtroom doors opened. Gregory and Darla, cuffed and bound with elemental restraints, came ahead of a coterie of guards.

Marcus' emotions went haywire, and Sophie sent calming life energy through him as she watched her in-laws walk toward the defense's table.

They caught Sophie's and Marcus' eyes as they passed. Gregory nodded subtly, and Darla smiled halfheartedly.

Then they took their seats, and the trial began.

Sophie started out hopeful, but as witness after witness came forward to testify against the Templetons, her hope dwindled. Gregory sat tall and unmoving throughout it all, but she could see his white-knuckled hand in Darla's and his thumb rubbing the back of his wife's hand to keep her calm.

Finally, the prosecution rested their case, and the courtroom sat in stunned silence.

"Does the defendant have anything to say?" the judge asked blandly as if he already knew the answer.

Marcus wiggled restlessly in his seat, but Sophie stilled him. They couldn't speak unless Gregory called them to the stand.

Darla peeked at Marcus, but Gregory, still facing forward, shook his head. He whispered something to Darla, whose face turned ashen. Then he leaned close to the microphone and cleared his throat.

"No, Your Honor," he answered simply.

The prosecution began to chatter quietly with smiles. They knew they'd won.

Marcus let out a whimper, then a choked sob. Sophie cradled him as he cried.

"Very well," the judge replied with a sigh. "Has the jury reached a verdict?"

There was a flurry of movement in the jury box. Then the lead juror stood up to the microphone and cleared his throat.

"Yes, Your Honor."

"Let's hear it," the judge intoned.

Sophie wept with Marcus as the jury's foreman seemed to speak for hours, listing charge after charge, many of them with a standard penalty of life in prison, all with a resounding "Guilty" at the end. She noticed that none of them contained Darla's name and wondered if Gregory had worked something out so that she could go free. Knowing him, it was likely. He'd orchestrated their entire career. He'd know how to orchestrate her freedom as well.

The jury finished, and the judge sighed.

"I think everyone here would agree there's only one sentence fitting for a criminal career so exhaustive," the judge snarled. He threw a contemptuous glance at Gregory, who didn't budge. "Gregory Raphael Templeton, you are hereby sentenced to judicial execution." He banged the gavel.

"No!" Marcus cried. He scrambled to his feet as the prosecution and the public seated behind them began to clap and cheer. "No!"

Sophie's breath left her as she and Robert numbly pulled Marcus back into his seat and wrapped their arms around him. She stared in shock as Gregory stood. He hauled an inconsolable Darla to her feet and pressed his hands against her face, speaking to her calmly and steadily.

"Why didn't you let us speak?" Marcus shouted.

Gregory and Darla turned as one to face him. They took a step closer, but security guards stopped them.

"No!" Marcus leapt up and shoved Sophie's and Robert's hands away. "Let me speak to them."

Sophie followed on his heels, and the security guards formed a tight circle around the four of them. "Three minutes. Then we have to take him," one of them grumbled.

"Why?" Marcus demanded of Gregory. "Why didn't you let us testify?"

"It wouldn't have stopped this from happening,"

Gregory noted in a monotone. "I didn't want to give you any inkling of false hope. I knew what was coming. I'm not afraid of it, Marcus." His amber eyes were earnest.

Marcus whirled on Darla. "Did you know? How could you let him do this?"

"Yes, darling." Darla sobbed. "I knew. Trust me. It doesn't make it any easier." She desperately clung to Gregory.

Marcus shook his head, clenching his eyes shut against more tears. Sophie clutched his hand, unable to stop her tears from streaming freely.

"Listen to me," Gregory soothed. He touched both their faces, his gaze flitting between them. "Stick with the plan. Defeat our enemy. I know you can. You will go on to live happy, whole lives, free of the curse." He smiled affectionately at them.

"I don't want to do it without you," Marcus choked, his voice barely a whisper. "I want you to be here with us."

"Darla will be here," Gregory noted. He pulled his wife close and kissed her forehead. "She will only spend another year in prison, and then she will go free. I made sure of it. You won't be alone." He took Darla's hands, then her face, and kissed her lips. "Watch our family grow, my love. Protect what we love most in this world. I know you will."

Darla clung to Gregory, her heart-wrenching sobs tearing Sophie apart.

Then Gregory turned to Sophie and Marcus.

Marcus wrapped Gregory in a hug. "I love you, no matter what you've done. I needed to tell you."

Sophie's heart broke as she watched Marcus shake with sobs against Gregory's shoulder. Gregory stroked Marcus' hair, eyes closed and brow furrowed against tears of his own. "I love you, my son. With all my heart."

Then Gregory opened his eyes and fixed her with his gaze.

Marcus let go, and Gregory stepped forward to clasp Sophie's hand.

"My dear girl," Gregory greeted softly. "Continue to shine bright. You are a light in this world. Never let yourself grow dim with hopelessness. You are never alone."

Sophie broke down, then hugged as Marcus had.

He stiffened for a second before hugging her back.

"Time's up." Hands pulled Gregory roughly out of Sophie's grasp.

Darla reached for him. "No! Let me go with him."

"My love, you must stay here," Gregory told her. The guards allowed him and Darla a final embrace and a kiss before they urged Gregory toward the back door of the courtroom.

Darla collapsed to her knees, and Sophie knelt beside her, followed by Marcus and Robert.

"It's okay," Marcus told his mother, though his voice broke. "It'll be okay." He wrapped an arm around her shoulder.

Darla wept. He pulled her into a hug and wept, too.

Sophie joined the group hug.

Robert looked on with shimmering eyes.

CHAPTER NINETEEN

The last weeks of July and the month of August ticked by under a haze of grief and apprehension. Gregory's sentence would be carried out in mid-September, and Marcus marked the date on their calendar with tears streaming down his cheeks. He'd offered to help Darla with the arrangements and to be there with her at Gregory's side when his final moment came.

Sophie felt his emotions as he glared at the calendar. Bitterness that Gregory was leaving this world just as he'd found a way into Marcus' heart. Anger at himself for not saying anything at the trial. Confusion. Didn't Gregory *want* to be part of his life? Why had he given himself up so readily? Why hadn't he *fought*? All of that, followed by resigned, grudging respect. Gregory was getting the justice he deserved when all was said and done, and he was facing it with honor and dignity, not running from it and not cowering in fear.

It was the best they could hope for.

Sophie's hope and strength were declining since the

task of keeping everyone's spirits high stole what little energy she had. Ten-hour days piled on top of one another, and as the last week of August came to a close, Sophie wobbled on her feet in Nurse Bonnie's office as the last patient left for the day. Her stomach roiled, and she steadied herself against the wall and swallowed acid.

"Girl." Charlotte swept Sophie's hair out of her eyes. "You gonna be okay?"

"I'm fine," Sophie rasped. "Just need something to eat. Not like I'll keep it down anyway." She let Charlotte wrap an arm around her waist and lead her toward Thicket Hall, past throngs of EBI agents and citizen elementals who'd come together to help. As they hobbled up the steps, Headmistress Rogers opened the double doors and gave Sophie a sympathetic look.

"There's plenty of food inside," she soothed. Her dark eyebrows slanted, and her eyes flashed. "I'm not sure the school year should start until the battle looming over us is done." She glanced at Sophie questioningly. "If there is any way we can make this happen sooner rather than later, I think we'd all be better off for it. Especially you."

Sophie studied the headmistress through tired, bleary eyes. "There is a way," she deadpanned. She glanced at Charlotte, who gave her a wary look. "Call a meeting with the Defenders. We'll discuss it."

The headmistress' eyes widened, then she nodded firmly. "I'll do it. Have everyone meet in the dining hall in ten minutes."

Sophie nodded, and the headmistress hurried up the spiral staircase to the faculty offices.

When she was out of sight, Sophie's shoulders slumped.

Her heart ached at the thought of Marcus taking what was left of Thicket Hall's life energy after they'd worked themselves to the bone trying to keep it alive. Still less did she relish the idea of her new husband becoming the Serpent's commander. She had no idea what might happen, and while she trusted Gregory's judgment and strategic ability, she worried about the effect it might have on Marcus.

"Let's feed you, girl." Charlotte towed her to a table, and Sophie sent out a group text, calling all the Defenders to Thicket Hall. Then she struggled to swallow the bland food Charlotte placed in front of her—banana bread, a bowl of rice, and an apple.

"If I didn't know any better, I'd say you had one of those weird stomach bugs," Charlotte noted as she watched Sophie gag.

"No." Sophie sighed and shook her head. "It feels different. I'll be hungry one second, then so sick I can't see straight the next. I've been waking up in the middle of the night, too. Weird dreams are waking me up at 4 AM, and not even snuggles with Marcus help."

She shook her head, then leaned close to Charlotte's ear. "I'm a wreck, Char. How am I supposed to fight in this shape? How am I supposed to inspire hope and confidence when I'm seasick?" As if to punctuate her point, a wave of nausea washed over her, raising goosebumps on her arms. She struggled to retain the food she'd just eaten and clamped her hands over her mouth with a shudder.

Charlotte pulled her hair back from her face, then rubbed her back comfortingly. Her brown eyes held a question as she studied Sophie.

"It could be the stress, girl," Charlotte noted after a

moment had passed and Sophie's stomach settled enough for her to nibble more rice. She leaned close. "Let me ask you something, though. Have you had...you know, that time of the month?"

Sophie furrowed her brows. "Um." She stifled a burp, then shuddered again. "I'm not sure." As she racked her brain, thinking through the last several weeks, she couldn't remember the last time she'd had her cycle. It had been late before her wedding due to the anxiety of making sure everything went according to plan. It was possible that was happening again because of her stress about what was to come. "Gee. I guess I'm so stressed it's messing up my body's rhythms."

Charlotte's brow furrowed as something solidified in her mind. Sophie could tell by the determined twinkle in her eyes.

"Girl. You don't think..." Charlotte eyed her suspiciously, then gave a teasing grin.

Sophie studied her, bewildered. "Don't think what? I'm so confused."

Charlotte laughed, then opened her mouth to elaborate, but Simon's voice rang out from the doors of Thicket Hall.

"We're here!" He hurried in, with Janet right beside him.

"It was hard to get away," Janet explained breathlessly. "Had a problem with one of the roots."

Sophie glanced quizzically at Charlotte, but she shook her head and pursed her lips.

"Later. We'll talk later."

Sophie nodded weakly, then watched as Olivia and Cedric made their way inside. Marcus followed, and as he met Sophie's gaze, he frowned worriedly and hurried to her side.

"You look like a ghost," he began, draping his arm over her shoulders. "Did you eat something?"

"A little," Sophie admitted. She rested her head on his shoulder. "I feel awful."

"I'm sorry, princess." He rubbed between her shoulder blades and kissed her forehead. "I wish I could send you home, but I can't come take care of you."

"Mom or Dad would," Sophie put in.

Headmistress Rogers hurried down the stairs as the Defenders gathered at the table. "Good, you're all here. Miss Briggs…I mean, Agent Jenkins suggested that there's a way to speed this process along. As you know, the beginning of the school year is approaching fast, and I don't want students on campus until the Serpent's threat is neutralized."

Sophie shivered alongside the others as their yellow-orange Defender magic flared in protest.

The headmistress sheepishly covered her mouth. "My apologies."

"Happens all the time," Cedric joked.

"Can someone explain how we can start the battle on our time? Is it true? Is it possible?" the headmistress asked.

Marcus sighed, then glanced at Sophie. "You told her, huh?"

She nodded weakly. "I think she's right. I think it's for the best if we get this over with. It's stealing our energy and our hope to keep waiting like this."

Marcus studied her earnestly. "Are you sure you're okay with it?"

Sophie heaved a resigned sigh. "I don't think we have a choice anymore."

Marcus nodded grimly. He beckoned for Charlotte and Janet to sit next to Sophie to support her, then stood next to Headmistress Rogers.

"What's this all about, Prince Death?" Olivia snarked. "Why are we always the last to know what you two are scheming?"

Marcus chuckled humorlessly. "We haven't said anything because you guys aren't gonna like it. It might be our last best shot, though."

"Okay." Simon crossed his arms and studied Marcus. "We can handle it."

"We've been through hell and back plenty of times," Cedric noted. "We can do it one more time."

Sophie smiled weakly. It did her heart good to see her fellow Defenders' trust and hope.

Marcus nodded. "All right. Here goes."

He launched into Gregory's plan, and their friends' faces went pale with apprehension. The headmistress studied him with an unreadable expression as he talked.

"So, let me get this straight," Olivia began once Marcus had finished. "You gotta kill Thicket Hall just like you tried to your freshman year. Then you're gonna control the snake thing?"

Marcus nodded. "Something like that."

"I don't like it," Janet snapped. She studied Marcus. "What if she turns the tables on you? What if she controls you instead, or she messes with your head to turn you against us?"

"Gregory said that wouldn't happen," Marcus assured

her. "He encountered that thing before, remember? He knows what she's like. He protected me from her. Besides, if I *don't* have control of her, she'll keep attacking me, especially if Connor gets to her first."

Cedric nodded. "I think it's clever. Not ideal, but very clever. Leave it to your dad to think up something like this."

Marcus smiled halfheartedly at him. "Yep."

"Well." Headmistress Rogers spoke at last. She studied Marcus, then the rest of the Defenders. "It seems we need to call in our reinforcements. We must have everything ready to go for the final battle. Then we can implement this plan with the rest of the Defenders on standby to make sure you won't fall to some unforeseen obstacle."

Marcus nodded in understanding. "Just name the time and day."

"Today. Now." The headmistress' eyes flashed. "I'll begin calling the army together. In the meantime, rest and eat. Gather your strength." Her hands flashed fire. "This threat to our school and our lives ends today."

Sophie's magic flared in response to the headmistress' courage and determination. She nodded in tandem with the other Defenders, who'd gone still and quiet.

It was going to end today.

CHAPTER TWENTY

Over the next couple of hours, EBI agents poured onto the campus. Her parents and sister showed up, alongside dozens of other worried adults, and they gathered within Thicket Hall and around its bulk, chattering worriedly, fear and apprehension in their eyes.

Sophie choked down more food as the other Defenders directed the flow of people to various locations around the campus and the great tree. As she sat alone, trying to get one more bite of apple down without gagging, a gentle hand rested on her shoulder.

"You look like death," stated a familiar male voice.

She turned to see Mikey Carlisle standing behind her, looking worried.

She chuckled. "Yeah. I feel like it, too."

"What's got you feeling so awful?" Mikey asked. He sat next to her and flipped his blue-tipped hair out of his eyes. "Not gonna lie. I don't like that we're doing this with you in this shape."

"I don't like it either, but we don't have a choice,"

Sophie muttered. "If Marcus doesn't take control of the enemy, Connor will, and we have no idea where he is or what his plans are. We can't wait any longer. Besides, I've been sick for days. I don't think it'll stop until this stress goes away."

"For sure," Mikey agreed, his eyes sad as he watched her nibble on the apple. "I just wish there was something we could do to help you."

"If I could keep food down, that would be helpful," Sophie noted bitterly.

Mikey pressed his hand to her forehead and closed his eyes, focusing. Sophie felt gentle tendrils of death magic loosen her tight shoulders and work through the queasy knots in her stomach. Then he let go, and Sophie took a deep breath.

She smiled gratefully at him. "Thanks." She took a bite of her apple, pleased that she didn't immediately feel like hurling it back up. "Wow. That helped a lot."

"I've helped Nurse Bonnie on occasion this summer," Mikey told her smugly. "Bet you didn't know death elementals could heal."

"Actually, I did." Sophie chuckled. "Marcus helped me recover from a blast of life magic in Combat training. That was the first time I realized it." She smiled at Mikey. "You'd make a great nurse."

"Nah. I still want to be an astrophysicist." He laughed, then got up and patted her shoulder. "I need to go find Sabrina. She's probably freaking out, and I got the magic touch to calm her down." He pulled a bit of death magic into his palms and smirked as Sophie chuckled.

"Thanks for your help. Maybe now I can get some energy back," Sophie told him as he turned to leave.

"Can't have our angel of hope throwing up on the battlefield," Mikey teased. Then he saluted, winked, and hurried out of the dining hall.

Sophie ate half the banana bread and rice, then downed the mug of lukewarm coffee Charlotte had left her. It immediately did its work, rushing through her veins and filling her with much-needed energy.

Her stomach stayed calm as she breathed deeply, willing it all to stay down. Then she got up, hope rising in her heart.

It was time for her to join the others and prepare for the battle.

She headed to the back of Thicket Hall, where she'd been told to meet the other Defenders. They glanced at her in surprise as she greeted them with a smile.

"Weren't you just about to hurl?" Olivia snarked.

"You actually have some color now." Marcus looked relieved. He stepped up to her and smoothed her hair back. "What happened?"

"Well, *mon cher*, I got some help from an old friend." She glanced at the water building, where Mikey and Sabrina stood close together, talking. "Apparently, death magic can soothe nausea."

Marcus followed her line of vision and smiled. "Good to know." He hugged her. "I'm just happy to see you smiling again."

Glad you are better, Thicket Hall stated weakly in their minds. *Need you. All of you. Is time.*

Sophie pulled the acorn from her pocket and studied its cracking form sadly. *Time for what?* she asked, though she knew what the answer would be.

A distant howl rang through the air. The campus-wide chattering stopped, and a heavy stillness descended.

Marcus. Do it now, Thicket Hall urged. *Connor comes. No time to lose.*

Marcus' face paled, and he glanced at Sophie.

She took his hands, heart racing. "You can do this. You're not the bad guy, Marcus. You never have been. You're doing this so that the real bad guy can't win, okay?" She stood on tiptoe and pressed a kiss to his cheek. "I trust you. I believe in you."

"So do we." Simon stepped up and clapped Marcus' shoulder, followed by Janet, Cedric, and Olivia.

"You got this, Prince Death," Olivia affirmed.

Marcus drew strength from their trust and confidence. He took a deep breath and closed his eyes, then drew out his radio.

With trembling hands, he pressed the side button and spoke. "Trev. It's a go. We're doing this now."

The crackling response came back immediately. "Copy that, Jenkins. We trust you."

Marcus tucked the radio back into his pocket. Then he turned to the massive oak, tears welling in his eyes.

I don't want to do this, he told Thicket Hall as he approached its familiar but now-graying trunk.

Know it, I do. Thicket Hall's soothing response washed over him like a gentle warm rain. *This is only way you protect what you love. Strong power you have, but even bigger heart. Remember, I am not gone. I will come back when fight is over. First you must win fight. You must do this.*

Marcus nodded. He glanced over his shoulder as the wolves' baying came closer.

Tears ran down his cheeks as he dug deep for the power to kill, then sent his swirling, oily death magic into Thicket Hall.

I love you, you old grump, he sobbed.

Love you much, sapling, Thicket Hall replied tenderly. *Do this, you can. You must.*

Heart breaking, Marcus began to pull Thicket Hall's pitiful life energy out.

Sophie huddled with the other Defenders as Thicket Hall's dim gold glow disappeared into Marcus' death siphon. She'd heard their conversation, and tears ran down her cheeks as what color remained in its gray bark drained.

Marcus held one hand out, the magic in his hands a mixture of grim death and weak life. Then he closed his fingers into his fist and pulled his arm to his chest in a sharp motion, mimicking the gesture Gregory Templeton had made when he took Caleb Justice's life.

Thicket Hall's familiar rumbling quieted, then faded to nothing.

Sophie let out a choked sob. She'd known it was coming, but she wasn't prepared for the silence in her head and the gaping hole in her heart.

Janet hugged her. "Steady, girl." Her eyes were wet with tears behind her glasses.

Wolves howled like mad near the hill where Roscoe's barn towered above the campus. The Defenders turned as a hulking figure reached the top of the hill and cried out in rage.

"No! You can't do that!" Connor's familiar growl echoed across the campus.

The EBI agents gathered around the perimeter of the tree murmured.

"Actually, I can," hissed an oddly familiar otherworldly voice that made Sophie's hackles rise.

Sophie turned back to Thicket Hall and squeaked in terror. The other Defenders backed up by instinct, and Janet pulled Sophie with her when she refused to move.

Marcus, bathed in a rainbow glow, stood with his arms crossed, glaring at Connor with prismatic eyes and a wicked smirk.

"Rules are rules, my dear Connor," Marcus continued. Then he turned back to Thicket Hall and began to chant. The glow around his body got stronger, and the ground trembled.

"Oh, sugar honey iced tea," Janet muttered, her eyes flashing yellow gold. "I can feel it in the earth. She's coming to the surface. He's calling her up."

Sophie trembled as she watched Marcus lift his arms. His voice moved in slithering, lilting patterns.

The earthquake under their feet intensified, and Sophie took a deep breath and rubbed her arms.

Everything was going to plan. Marcus clearly had control of the Serpent and was calling her to the surface.

She had to prepare the Defenders and all their allies for the fight of their lives.

She closed her eyes and chanted her mantra. *Defenders are better together.* Janet gasped, and her friends released her as she transformed. Warmth burst against her skin, and as she opened her eyes, she launched into the air, buoyed by the awed stares of her Defender allies and the army that had gathered on the campus.

"Our enemy is coming!" Sophie declared, her tinkling voice echoing across the grounds. Hundreds of eyes locked onto her, taking in every word. "We have to hope. We have to fight! Whatever happens, *don't* let her steal your hope. We have gained control over her. The battle is ours to win!"

Cheers erupted alongside Connor's enraged shout. The Defenders morphed into their pure elemental forms as the ground split near Thicket Hall's roots.

"So, it's a battle you want, little fairy?" Connor roared. He lifted his chin. "I might not have Azdaja, but I have an army of my own. We'll see whose is better."

Howls and spine-tingling snarls echoed through the trees. Murmurs and gasps spread through the Defenders' army.

"We're not afraid of you!" Sophie shouted to alleviate their panic. "We will defeat you."

The Defenders and their army roared in affirmation. Sophie caught a glimpse of her little sister's dark, wavy hair and her ebullient cries of courage, and her heart swelled, her gold glow burning more brightly.

For Millie. For their future. For the future of everyone who ever hoped to attend the School of Roots and Vines and for the elemental and non-elemental worlds, they had to fight and win.

As long as Sophie could keep their spirits up and give them hope, they would be the victors.

CHAPTER TWENTY-ONE

Sophie's hope-filled words coursed through Marcus' veins alongside the thrumming, hair-raising energy of the Serpent's presence. The words hissing from his mouth tasted foreign and dark and left a burning sensation on his tongue. He had no idea what was happening anymore, but as always, Sophie was his anchor, his North Star, her warmth calling him back to himself and keeping him there.

A shudder raced through him as the ground split between his feet. The urge to run away blazed in his abdomen, but he was locked in place. He couldn't move until he'd accomplished his task and Azdaja stood before him in all her chaotic fearsomeness.

He heard Connor's fierce battle cry behind him.

Then the earth shook. He stepped to one side of the chasm and watched in mute terror as shimmering rainbow scales came toward him. Massive claws with tips like blades gouged the ground as the Serpent hauled herself out of the channels and into the surface realm. Leathery translucent wings the size of basketball courts spread wide, revealing a long, serpentine body that coiled and writhed in the sun.

A grinning dragon-like face and burning prismatic eyes towered over Marcus. Her nostrils blew smoke into Marcus' face, and scaly lips rose in a snarl, revealing fangs as long as one of Thicket Hall's boughs.

Terrified screams erupted behind Marcus.

"It's the Serpent!" a woman cried.

"Run!" someone else shouted.

Marcus clenched his trembling hands and held his ground.

"So," Azdaja hissed. Her voice echoed in the air and his mind, alien and rough like static. Her eyes flashed as she leaned down to study him. "*You* are my master this time, little Templeton. Interesting." Slithering laughter rumbled in her chest.

Marcus gulped as he faced Azdaja. "You will do as I say," he declared, willing his knees not to give out.

"Yes, of course." Azdaja sent her forked tongue between her teeth and sniffed the air as if looking for someone else. "Where is your blushing bride?"

Marcus' veins blazed with rage. "That's none of your concern." He flicked a surreptitious gaze at the sky, noting with relief that Sophie was gone. Then he forced himself to step toward Azdaja. Glittering reins appeared in his hands as the determination to take control of her pulsed through him.

She didn't move away as he approached and clambered onto her back. The reins curled around her snout and forelegs.

Azdaja growled, and the sound vibrated her body and Marcus' legs.

"Clever little Templeton," she hissed, turning her head to fix him with one burning eye. "You think the curse will be broken by your father's ploy. You are wrong."

He lifted his chin. "You're not going to make me second-guess him. *I'm* the one in control." He pulled the reins to turn her head away from him.

In response, she hurtled into the fray, sending agents and civilians scattering in terror. Her tongue flicked out, tasting the air, but Marcus jerked hard on the reins and yanked her to a stop.

"You're not going to hurt my army," he snarled.

"Why would I want to do that?" Azdaja replied levelly. "I have a different objective in mind."

"What objective?" Marcus demanded.

In response, Azdaja laughed. Her prismatic eyes found Sophie high in the air, heading for Connor and his wolf army, who were busily fighting a slew of EBI agents.

The rainbow flashing in her eyes turned red as her unblinking gaze followed Sophie. She licked her lips, then took off across campus after her.

"No!" Marcus roared and yanked on the reins. "You will *not* hurt her!"

Azdaja roared but kept going. "You have no power over the curse," she snarled.

"The curse? There's no curse on Sophie!" Marcus poured his rage through his hands and into the reins, and Azdaja howled in pain and dropped to the ground, writhing.

Marcus struggled to stay on her back. "She's not the one you want," he declared through clenched teeth. "I am."

Azdaja's howls tapered off. Then a low laugh slithered from her throat, sending shudders down Marcus' back. "What a fool you are."

Then she lunged toward Sophie again, beating her wings to rise into the air.

"Stop it! You are *not* going to hurt her!" Marcus insisted. He clutched the reins for dear life and squeezed Azdaja with his legs to keep from falling off.

"Marcus!"

Marcus craned his head toward the howling male voice that had called his name. Cedric, whipping around in a vast vortex, hovered nearby.

"Don't just tell her what *not* to do, man," Cedric advised. "Remember Caleb's legendarium?"

"Give her something to do," Marcus recalled softly. "Then she won't be able to go after Sophie until the task is complete."

Azdaja growled and flew faster, but Marcus eyed the wolves Sophie and the other Defenders were fighting.

"Azdaja!" he cried, yanking the reins. "Kill the wolves and their commander."

Azdaja shrieked in protest, but the reins in Marcus' hands glowed with blinding intensity.

"Do it! I am your master!" Marcus demanded.

The Serpent growled in defeat and plummeted toward the battle.

Sophie landed alongside Janet, Simon, and Olivia as they cornered Connor near Roscoe's barn.

"Well, well, snake charmer," Olivia hissed, her voice crackling like fire. "What are you gonna do without your precious dragon?"

"Seems to me you're up a creek without a paddle," Simon added.

Connor's steely blue eyes narrowed as he glanced at the four Defenders. "I always got a paddle," he retorted. His eyes flashed red-orange, and flames erupted all over him.

"No!" Olivia growled. "He's taking on my powers."

"Get back, you flaming devil!" A familiar voice made Sophie gasp.

"Pete, no!"

Peter charged up the hill at Connor, his hands filled with water magic. Sophie gaped before realizing it was likely the effect the Serpent's presence was having on *everyone* outside of the Defenders. It lined up with what the rock creature had shown her in its memory—elementals trying to use their magic but having it react in unexpected ways.

Mikey, Luke, and Vince followed in Peter's wake, shouting battle cries, their hands alight with life, earth, and death power, respectively.

Sophie shook her head with an incredulous laugh. Despite not having their own magic, they were taking it in stride and courageously charging into battle.

Still, they were putting themselves in *way* too much danger. They weren't trained to use elemental magic besides their own. They'd be weaker.

"Guys, no!"

Before Sophie or the others could stop them, they'd descended on Connor, knocking him to the ground. Luke desperately tried to form himself into a human rock shield for the other boys.

Simon hurriedly doused them all with water to help put out Connor's flames, but Connor roared and blasted wind magic next.

All four boys flew over their heads, screaming.

"Janet, quick!" Sophie cried.

Janet curled her hands and lifted. The earth trembled, softened, and rose to catch the boys, and they landed on the grass. As Sophie ran to help them, she realized all four were unconscious. Peter had a bleeding wound to the head. Mikey slumped over Vince with a massive red burn on his arm, and Luke groaned and twitched in pain.

"Oh, no," Sophie muttered. She touched each boy's forehead and sent life energy through them. Mikey's burn shifted from bright red to pink as Sophie swiped his blue-tipped hair out of his eyes. Peter's wound closed when she pressed her hands to his face.

"I'm so sorry," she whispered. "You guys are absolute warriors."

"Help!" Olivia's panicked cry rang out behind her. "Miracle Grow! All hands on deck!"

Sophie regretfully turned away from the boys to find Connor lashing Janet and Olivia with blinding whips of life energy. Cedric and Simon were battling hard to save the girls, but Connor growled and sent them hurtling away with wind magic, using two elements at once.

Sophie gasped. It seemed his limit on using one power at a time was gone due to the Serpent's presence.

She glanced at the wounded, unconscious boys, then at the shrieking girls who, though not falling to Connor's power, writhed in agony as it coursed through them.

Her grief and fear for their safety solidified into righteous fury. It blazed through her like summer sunlight, warming every inch of her with feverish heat.

How *dare* Connor hurt her friends?

Sophie ran back to Roscoe's barn, forming a fierce red-tinged ball of light between her hands. She launched it at Connor with a yell, and it hit him in the chest. "Put them down, you monster! Your reign of terror ends here!"

Connor dropped the girls as her life energy arced like raging lightning around his limbs. He collapsed to his knees with a howl of pain.

Simon growled and knocked him flat with a tidal wave of water. "Don't ever touch my girl again."

Janet struggled up, sucking in breaths, and slugged Connor in the nose with a crystalline fist as he tried to get to his hands and knees. "That's for making me a fossil in Mammoth Cave!" she shouted triumphantly.

Connor shrieked and covered his nose, but Olivia didn't give him time to recover before she hauled him up and pinned him to Roscoe's barn with a flaming hand.

"You're done, dragon man," she snarled. "You're done."

Cedric whirled beside her in his vortex and made her flames climb higher. "Got that right, queen."

A shriek above them made them all shudder, then glance at the sky.

The Serpent soared overhead. Black flames blasted from her mouth to the ground, charring her wolves to dust.

Connor chuckled, turned to air, and slipped out of Olivia's grasp.

"Get him!" Sophie pointed after him, but the Serpent landed in front of her, forcing her to step back.

"Kill the host!" she heard Marcus cry from Azdaja's back. "I command you!"

Azdaja shrieked again, and Sophie clamped her hands over her ears as the sound threatened to tear her apart from the inside out.

The Serpent tore after Connor's whirlwind, chasing him past the greenhouse to the tree line at the edge of campus. He shifted back to himself and stumbled as Marcus lashed him with a whip of death energy, then he toppled to the ground. The Serpent towered over him.

"Don't listen to him!" Connor pleaded. "He's—"

Sophie shuddered and covered her eyes as an anguished cry rang through the air, then abruptly cut off.

"Your command has been executed, Master," Azdaja snarled.

Sophie gulped. Connor was dead. She saw the Defenders' army regrouping, healing one another, and picking each other up off the ground. There wasn't a single wolf in sight.

Her heart was buoyed with hope. Marcus had used Azdaja against her own army. He'd made her slaughter all the wolves and Connor, leaving them with only the Serpent herself. With Marcus in control of her, she couldn't hurt anyone. They could send her back to the realm of chaos without a protest from her.

Their plan was working beautifully.

She ran toward the unconscious boys with the other Defenders at her side. They stirred as she knelt beside them.

"What happened?" Peter mumbled. He pressed his hand to his forehead with a wince.

"You were playing the hero, like always," Sophie teased him. She helped him sit up and ruffled his sandy hair, and he grinned at her.

"Ouch, that burn looks awful," Olivia commented as she scanned Mikey's arm. "Green, you want to put some cold water on this?"

"On it." Simon covered Mikey's burn with his translucent hand.

"Feels much better already." Mikey sighed in relief.

"Luke? Vince? You guys okay?" Janet tugged both boys up, and Cedric dusted off their clothes with a gust of wind.

"Sophie!" Millie ran up the hill toward her, followed by Walter and Joyce.

She pulled them all into a hug.

"Is the fight over?" Walter eyed the tree line, where Marcus led Azdaja in circles, not letting her come close to them.

"Not quite," Sophie answered. "The hardest part is over, though. I think."

"I can't imagine being brave enough to ride a dragon like that," Millie remarked.

"I'm sure you could if the people you loved were

counting on you." Sophie ruffled her hair, and Millie beamed at her.

"You're right. I bet I could."

Sophie chuckled. "That's the spirit."

"Whoa!" Marcus' startled cry, followed by the whoosh of wings flapping, made them all stop and look up.

The Serpent was flying toward Sophie.

CHAPTER TWENTY-TWO

Sophie quickly formed a life shield. "Go! All of you! Get out of here!"

"Sissy, we can't just leave—"

"Go now!" Sophie shot her father a frantic look.

He grimaced in protest, but Joyce squeezed his shoulder. He grabbed Millie, and the three of them ran, followed by Mikey, Vince, Luke, and Peter.

Olivia, Simon, Janet, and Cedric stood beside Sophie and channeled their power through her, strengthening her life shield as Azdaja landed and snapped at her.

"Sophie! Get out of here!" Marcus shouted. He jerked the reins, every muscle in his body tense as he tried to keep Azdaja's snout away from Sophie's life shield. "I can't rein her in. I don't know why!"

Sophie frowned even as her body tensed in fear. Azdaja's teeth were like elephant tusks. "I can't just leave! We have to send her back to the realm of chaos."

"You humans are all idiots!" Azdaja hissed. Her grating, slithering voice was strained as she used all her strength to pull against Marcus. "You have no power over the curse. Nothing can break it. Nothing!"

"You will *not* hurt her!" Marcus protested. "I'm the youngest Templeton. It's me you want, and hurting her doesn't fulfill the curse."

Azdaja shrieked, stealing the breath from Sophie and nearly making her shield falter. She twisted, turned, and bucked, and Sophie watched in frozen terror as Marcus tried to hang on.

His prismatic reins snapped after another serpentine shriek, and he tumbled to the ground. He rolled and landed near Sophie's feet.

She pulled him to his feet, noting that the rainbow glow in his eyes had gone out.

Her stomach plummeted. "Marcus. I don't think you have control anymore."

His breath came in ragged gasps. "I think you're right."

Azdaja righted herself and fixed them with her fiery gaze.

Sophie redoubled her life shield as panic coursed through her veins.

"What now?" she squeaked.

"Got any other brilliant plans, Prince Death?" Olivia added.

"The six of us should be able to take her down," Marcus offered.

Azdaja slunk closer. "You thought you were going to outsmart me," she hissed. "I told you from the beginning that your little ploy was doomed to failure."

"We didn't fail," Simon retorted. "Your army is gone, and now you have to face all six Defenders."

Azdaja laughed. Goosebumps and an unpleasant crawling sensation pulsed through Sophie.

"Not even the full spectrum of elemental power can stop me from claiming my right," she growled. She fixed her flashing eyes on Sophie, and they went red again. "The new Mrs. Templeton is mine."

Sophie's blood ran cold as the others looked at her in confusion. Terror and adrenaline mingled in her veins. She couldn't piece her thoughts together to try to work out what Azdaja was saying.

"What does Sophie have to do with the curse?" Marcus demanded, asking the question Sophie couldn't verbalize herself.

"More than you know." Azdaja stepped closer, but Janet stepped in front of Sophie, her emerald form blazing with light.

"You're not gonna get her," Janet declared.

"Damn right, you're not." Marcus transformed into a shadowy silhouette and locked arms with Janet. Simon, Olivia, and Cedric joined them.

Sophie, empowered by their fearlessness, let her life shield blaze bright and covered them all in a gold dome of protection.

Azdaja studied Sophie. Her huge teeth scraped Sophie's life shield, but it held firm.

"Fine," Azdaja hissed. "Stay in your little bubble of protection." She backed up, then flapped her wings. "We'll see how long you can bear to watch as your precious school and your army go up in flames."

Sophie choked. "No."

"I will get what I am due, one way or another," Azdaja warned as she soared into the sky.

"Stay put," Olivia told Sophie. Her glowing eyes were firm, though she glanced sadly at the sky. "We can't put her back in the realm of chaos without you."

"I can't just let her destroy the school," Sophie protested. Her hands shook with indecision. "I can't let her hurt everyone. My mom and dad and sister are out there!"

"So are mine," Olivia shot back. "They're all here fighting for *you*. If you give up and let this dragon have you, what's to stop her from hurting everyone anyway?"

"We have to stop her," Simon put in. "Maybe Cedric can get us into the air, or maybe we can get her back on the ground and fight her."

"Yes. We have to draw her back to fight *us* instead of attacking the others," Janet added. She glanced at Sophie. "Let your shield down. Call her back, and see if she'll take the bait. Then we fight."

"I think that's our best shot," Cedric agreed.

Sophie nodded, then exchanged glances with Marcus.

He blinked, then nodded once.

Sophie let her shield down and stood in front of the others. "Azdaja!" she cried, grimacing as the name slipped off her tongue like oil. "Come back! I'm here."

The massive beast, soaring like a vulture over the school while people ran for cover, glided back toward Sophie. Her wings blew the waters of the pond at the water elemental building, and Sophie prayed no one was inside.

As the Serpent landed, pummeling them with air from her wings, Sophie resisted the urge to cringe into Marcus' arms. He stood directly behind her, his chill comforting against her warmth.

"Well." Azdaja lowered her scaly head toward Sophie and sent a puff of smoky air into her face. "How magnanimous of you to give yourself up for your friends. I'll expect your Defender friends to back off unless they'd like to be destroyed with you."

Marcus stood beside Sophie and took her hand. His eyes blazed in challenge.

"We're not going anywhere. If you want Sophie, you have to fight us for her," Olivia declared. She stood beside Marcus, and Simon, Janet, and Cedric stood on Sophie's other side.

Azdaja's eyes burned bright. "Very well. Have it your way." She shrieked, then slashed with a massive claw. Olivia and Marcus fell under the blow, and before Sophie could conjure her magic to react, she'd done the same to Simon, Janet, and Cedric. They all sprawled on the ground, leaving Sophie standing alone.

"Guys!" Sophie cried, then glanced at Simon, who'd changed back to his human form and clutched his chest. A dark, muddy stain spread under his fingers. Janet's drenched hair stuck to her face, and she weakly coughed up water. Cedric lay panting and staring blankly at the sky, his creamy skin splotched with bright red burns.

Olivia looked like she'd been through a hurricane and lay shivering and muttering nonsense.

Marcus lay still and colorless at Sophie's feet, twitching under arcing life energy.

Sophie stared at Azdaja and choked. She'd used their opposite element to stun them all and trigger them out of their Defender forms.

"Now, then, my sweet," Azdaja purred. "Come here quietly, and I'll think about killing you quickly."

Sophie let life energy pool in her hands and formed a shield around her friends. "Don't you dare hurt them anymore," she snarled.

"Oh, I won't," Azdaja crooned. "It's you I want." She circled Sophie with a menacing chuckle.

"Why?" Sophie demanded. She gulped back tears and tried to quiet her pounding heart. "Tell me why, and I'll let you have me. Is it because I married Marcus? Does that make me the youngest Templeton? Or are you just trying to get to him so he'll surrender?"

"Making demands, are we?" Azdaja stopped in front of her. "Very well. I'm in a generous mood today, having outsmarted my centuries-old enemy for the fifteenth time. I'll tell you why your precious husband and friends will die in vain trying to save you."

Her prismatic eyes glittered as she lowered her head to Sophie's level. "It's true that yours is not Templeton blood. Marrying into the family doesn't impart the curse to you. However, the Templeton line is continued—and *carried*—by those who marry into it."

Sophie blinked, trying to puzzle through her words. "Okay. So Darla isn't part of the curse, but Gregory and Marcus are."

"How clever you are," Azdaja purred. "You still are not clever enough to put the pieces together, though. *So* sad.

You will die in despair, not knowing why." She towered over Sophie and opened her great mouth.

Sophie extended her life shield over herself, earning her a growl from the Serpent.

"You said you would tell me first," Sophie hissed. "Explain it to me. Spell it out. I need to know." She felt Marcus stirring at her feet and took a deep breath. If she could keep the snake talking, maybe she could find a way to strengthen her fellow Defenders and get them back on their feet.

"Are you really so stupid?" Azdaja curled around her life shield, forcing Sophie to use all her strength to keep it intact. "Humans really are good for nothing. Surely you aren't blind to the truth." The Serpent leered at Sophie. "You carry the youngest Templeton within you, the accursed child of an accursed union. I can smell his blood. It calls to me. *That* is why you must die."

CHAPTER TWENTY-THREE

Sophie's thoughts ground to a standstill. She gasped, and her breaths came in short, ragged bursts. She put her shaking hands against her tummy.

"W-what?" she managed to squeak.

Had Azdaja just said she was *pregnant*?

Azdaja cackled in triumph as Sophie's life shield weakened, cracking under the weight of her confused emotions.

"Darling girl!" a familiar high-pitched female voice yelled across the grass. "Darling girl, what are you doing? Fight!"

Sophie gaped in disbelief as a familiar blonde figure darted across the grass toward her, followed by the tall, dashing figure of Sophie's father-in-law and a coterie of guards.

Apparently, they'd let the Templetons out to join the fray. Things must have looked desperate for the EBI to approve that.

"Ah, the grinning grandparents join the party." Azdaja

chuckled. "Now the whole family can perish at once, like they should have nineteen years ago."

The Templetons froze and stared at Sophie. "Did she just say 'grandparents?'" Darla squeaked.

Sophie gazed at them, as shocked as they looked.

Gregory's eyes softened as he searched Sophie's face for confirmation. Seeing nothing but shock, he gave a haunted smile and a nod. Then his eyes blazed silver with rage, and he turned to the Serpent.

"You will not do to this young family what you did to ours!" Gregory shouted at Azdaja. He dissolved into a shadow, then conjured a death vortex and shielded Sophie from Azdaja's view.

Darla called up her magic too, but it came into existence as fire in her palm, the chaotic loosened channels working their mischief. She shrieked and shook it off her hand, then took Gregory's arm and lent him her strength instead.

Apparently, the Defenders—and former Defenders—were the only ones immune to Azdaja's topsy-turvy effect on elemental magic.

Sophie trembled. It was too much at once. She was going to have a baby. She and Marcus were going to be parents, but for that to happen, she had to win this fight.

A hand grasped for Sophie's, and she glanced down to see Marcus on his knees, staring up at her, his bruised and dirty face streaked with tears.

When she glanced past the downed Defenders, she saw a massive crowd approaching—their army. Their shouts echoed across the grass. *"You can't have her! You can't have her!"*

Her sister Amelia led the chant. Emily, the new girl they'd met, stood beside her. Peter and the guys and Charlotte and Leslie flanked her.

"Sophie," Marcus rasped. "We have to keep fighting. We *have* to." His trembling hand rested on her stomach, and his eyes showed a fierce, protective love. "It's not just us anymore."

Sophie's lips trembled.

"We have to keep going for the innocent, the unborn, the new students, and the generations to come after us," Marcus continued. He hugged her belly and kissed it tenderly. "We need your hope and love now, Sophie. We gotta protect what we love, and you gotta let them protect what they love." He gestured at the chanting crowd, then smiled weakly at her.

Sophie hugged Marcus and sobbed. Joy, hope, and furious maternal love spread through her like wildfire.

She let it pull her into the air and swirl around her like sunlight through fog. Then she gathered all her courage, hope, and love into her hands, formed a sun-like orb of life energy, and sent it toward the ground.

It broke and coursed through the campus, starting with the Templetons and the Defenders. The light gave them the strength to get back to their feet. Darla's battle cries grew fiercer, and Gregory's silhouette glowed as he blocked Azdaja's attempts to get past him.

When the light touched over her army, they shouted and cheered and rallied around the Defenders and the Templetons.

"Defenders!" Marcus cried. He paced the grass between the Defenders and their army. "Allies! Friends and family!"

They roared in response.

"For all that's good and beautiful and innocent in this world, for all we hope for, will we give up, or will we fight this last battle and *win*?"

The crowd chanted, "Fight and win! Fight and win!"

The Defenders morphed into their elemental forms. Marcus cast a tender glance at Sophie before he melted into shadow.

Sophie touched down and spread her arms.

"Life elementals, join me! Death elementals, join Marcus! Everyone find your Defender and stick with them. This is the final battle, and we'll need *everyone's* strength to get through it. Are you ready?"

Her army's affirmative roar was deafening. They gathered around the Defenders, channeling their energy through each until their glows rivaled the sun.

Sophie, standing in the massive pool of energy from her fellow life elementals, smiled at Charlotte on her left side and ruffled Millie's hair on her right.

"Let's make the biggest shield known to man!" she exclaimed.

"Go for it, girl," Charlotte urged.

Sophie swirled energy between her hands, then sent the resulting huge gold ball into the air with a shout. It cascaded around the entire army like a sparkling curtain.

Azdaja charged it, snarling, but it held firm. Sophie barely felt the impact since she had the strength of dozens of life elementals at her beck and call.

"Give me the girl!" Azdaja roared.

Gregory, who'd pulled Darla inside the shield at the last

second, morphed out of his Defender form and hurried to stand in front of the Defenders.

"Not a chance," he snarled. Then he turned to the Defenders. "Listen to me," he began. "Each element needs to strike in order and in pairs. Earth and water, air and fire, death and life."

"That's right," Cedric confirmed. "I remember that from Uncle Caleb's legendarium. Each element pair has a different task to accomplish."

Gregory gave him a grim smile. "Your uncle was a top-notch researcher. It must bring you comfort to know that even now, he is helping us."

Cedric returned the smile. "Yeah."

"What part of her do earth and water need to hit?" Simon asked. He and Janet studied Gregory expectantly.

Gregory shook his head and glanced at Cedric, then at Marcus. "Those two have studied the legendarium. I haven't seen it in years."

Sophie felt the shivering sensation of Marcus' psionic presence. *Earth and water. Hmm. Water puts out the fire inside of her. Earth is supposed to "ground" her. Maybe something to do with her wings?*

Simon and Janet nodded thoughtfully, then glanced at each other and grinned.

"We got it," Janet affirmed. She took Simon's hand. "We'll need to step outside the shield to strike her. Can someone stun her for a second to give us an opening?"

"On it," Sophie replied. She conjured a vast life comet, then waited until Azdaja charged them again.

She stared the beast down, waiting for her to expose her torso.

Azdaja roared, and Sophie moved swiftly. She opened the shield enough for Janet and Simon to slip through, then launched her life comet at Azdaja's throat.

The Serpent's roar became a howl of pain, and her wings fanned out behind her as she writhed.

Janet let out a ferocious cry and sent a rain of razor-sharp gems at the snake. The earth elementals feeding her strength, including Pete and Trevor, roared in triumph as the gems shredded her leathery wings.

"You dirty little sneaks!" Azdaja screamed. Her huge claws gouged the ground as she tried to fold her perforated wings against her body.

Simon wasted no time. Using the energy from the water elementals, among them Colin and Leslie, he put his transparent hands together and formed a hose. The stream blasted into the Serpent's open, howling mouth. Smoke poured from her nostrils as she coughed and bellowed.

Simon yanked Janet back inside the shield as Azdaja raised a claw to strike them. Sophie quickly closed it behind them, then winced as the Serpent's claws struck the shield.

Azdaja crawled up and over their shield, shrieking.

"Don't let her scare you!" Sophie cried over the ruckus. "She can't get in unless we let fear weaken us!"

The army shouted battle cries.

"Great job, you guys," she told Janet and Simon as they resumed their places beside her. They beamed at her and gave each other a high five.

Cedric glanced at Olivia. "I guess we're up next, queen."

Olivia's eyes were on the Serpent, who tried desperately

to conjure her fire but came up with nothing but dark smoke.

"What are we supposed to do?" she asked. "I'm glad she can't fly or shoot fire anymore. What else can we do to weaken her?"

"This one I know," Cedric declared. "You're supposed to blind her, and I'm supposed to help."

"Interesting." Olivia gazed at Sophie. "You ready to let us out?"

"Be careful," Sophie advised. "If she wasn't angry before, she is now."

"Like I haven't dealt with my fair share of angry snakes." Olivia scoffed. She and Cedric walked arm in arm to the edge of the shield, Olivia's fiery hair blazing. Cedric's whirlwind was tight and strong.

Sophie reluctantly let them out.

"Again you come to taunt me?" Azdaja shrieked as she charged the pair.

Cedric moved first, and his whirlwind caught Azdaja's pierced wings. Sophie gaped as the trees on campus bent under the power of his gust and as the Serpent shrieked and rolled across the ground.

"That's how it's done, bro!" Bri shouted. Her eyes and those of the other air elementals glowed as they supplied energy to him.

Azdaja landed in a heap close to the edge of the shield, and Olivia stepped up, leapt onto her head, and plunged her flaming hands into the dragon's prismatic eyes.

"Fearless," Dottie shouted.

"That's my baby girl!" added Trisha, her glowing eyes welling with tears.

The Serpent uttered the most piercing shriek yet. Sophie gritted her teeth against the sound, then gasped as Olivia toppled off her head with a scream.

Cedric's vortex caught her, then whipped another gust at the Serpent as she tried to storm after them. Sophie hurriedly let them in and held the shield firm as Azdaja's claws raked it furiously.

"It's our turn," Gregory declared. "Death to send her back to the hell she came from." His eyes flashed silver as he took Darla's hand and glanced at Marcus.

Marcus nodded and swept toward the edge of the shield. His ghostly chill amplified as his eyes brightened from silver to white, and black tendrils undulated around him.

"Wicked, man," Mikey remarked, high-fiving Stephen and Vincent, who were standing beside him.

"Where are you, filthy humans?" Azdaja shrieked. "I can smell you."

Sophie opened the shield enough for Marcus to creep out silently. As soon as he'd set foot outside, Azdaja's face swiveled toward him.

"I smell a Templeton," she hissed.

"Oh, darling," Darla murmured, clinging to Gregory's arm. "I can hardly bear to watch."

Marcus pulled his hands apart, and a huge, net-like vortex of death magic spread between them.

He launched it at Azdaja. The amplified death magic covered her body like a spider's web and tightened.

Azdaja screamed and writhed. Gold life magic flared from her rainbow scales, trying to break the bonds.

Marcus redoubled his efforts. Sophie could hear the

grunts of the other death elementals as they fed him power.

"Take as much as you need, my son," Gregory called. "Defeat her! Break the curse. It's *your* victory this time!"

Azdaja fell onto her side. Her claw barely missed Marcus as she kicked and fought with all her strength.

Marcus stepped back and grew. Sophie saw prismatic energy flow into his death vortex as he siphoned it from Azdaja.

Then his psionic presence flared in her mind, frantic.

I can't take it all on. This is where you come in, princess.

"Quickly," Gregory urged Sophie, beckoning her toward the shield. "He needs you."

Sophie took a deep breath and nodded. She released the life shield, and her army gasped and murmured.

"It's all right," she assured them. "This battle is almost done."

She stepped forward and took Marcus' enlarged hand, then gasped and clenched her teeth. Chaotic mixed energy pulsed through her faster than she could keep up with it. She pushed it through herself and let each element surround her energy. It formed a rainbow around her gold glow, garnering awed murmurs from their army.

"Everyone!" she shouted. "Come to me and reach out. It's going to take us all to pull the magic from her."

"Elemental magic prism for the win," Simon shouted with a laugh. He and Janet ran forward with the water and earth elementals behind them to take green and turquoise magic from Sophie's supercharged form.

"Coming, sweetie!" Joyce, Millie, and Walter joined her

to take on the life magic that was making Sophie's hair stand on end. Charlotte and Emily weren't far behind, along with the other life elementals in the crowd. They formed a chain and began to glow gold as they reached toward Sophie.

"Well, Ced, I guess we'd better listen to Miss Miracles. She's done this before, after all," Olivia snarked.

"Darn right, Liv," Sophie teased.

Olivia rolled her eyes, then she and Cedric led the fire and air elementals to Sophie's side. Red-orange and silver-blue magic arced out of Sophie toward their outstretched hands.

"So this is what Caleb's power could have been. This is what we could have done together," Gregory murmured softly. He and Darla, with Mikey, Vincent, Stephen, and the other death elementals, crowded around Sophie with awed stares.

Sophie reached toward the Templetons, and they reached back with teary smiles. Death magic funneled from her fingertips to theirs, bathing them all in a silver glow.

"It's an honor to see this day," Gregory continued. "An honor to see you and my son working side by side. To think I'd live to see the day the curse would be broken, not for my son's sake, but for—"

"Darling," Darla cautioned. She cast a furtive glance at Sophie's parents, who stood a few yards away, oblivious to the conversation. "Perhaps we shouldn't speak of that now. Our son and daughter-in-law might want to announce it *themselves*. Later, you know. When we're not sending this worm back to hell."

Gregory pursed his lips, then nodded. "Perhaps you're right, dearest."

Sophie couldn't help but chuckle, and she felt the ripples of Marcus' psionic presence light up in her mind with his mirth.

Azdaja groaned, forcing their attention back to her. She whined as she weakened. Her massive claws and teeth were no longer a threat as she thrashed. Her rainbow sheen faded and darkened, and still the energy flooded through Marcus and Sophie.

Azdaja turned gray like Thicket Hall. She gave a last cry of defeat as Marcus' death magic overtook her like a shadow.

The river of magic stopped abruptly, and Sophie stumbled.

Marcus curled his fingers into a fist and jerked his arm to his chest—the killing blow.

A shimmering, shapeless blob of energy rose from Azdaja's head, glowing with all the colors of the rainbow. It dissipated, and her reptilian form disintegrated into black dust.

Sophie exhaled raggedly. "We did it."

The Serpent was dead.

CHAPTER TWENTY-FOUR

Sophie shot into the air, buoyed by her joy. "Azdaja is dead!"

A deafening roar rang out like victory bells. Everyone rushed forward to reach for Sophie's hands, and she obliged them with tears of joy running down her cheeks.

"We couldn't have done this without all of you," she noted, her tinkling, otherworldly voice lighting everyone's faces with radiant smiles. She hugged her sister and parents, tackled Charlotte in a hug, and laughed as her roommates and male friends drowned her in a group hug.

As she got to her feet, Charlotte gasped and pointed up.

"Sophie! Look!"

She squinted, trying to see where Charlotte was pointing.

A tiny glowing object was floating a few yards above her head. As she studied it, its identity clicked into place.

"Thicket Hall's acorn," she murmured. She jumped, using her Defender powers, and cupped the acorn in her palms.

It warmed, then floated toward the gray skeleton of Thicket Hall. The ground was still split in front of it, and as Sophie followed the acorn's tug, it paused over the roots and waited.

She studied it curiously. "Guys," she called to the Defenders. "I think we have one more job to do."

"That's correct," Gregory called from amid the excited chatter. He made his way to the front of the crowd as it quieted and gazed at her. "You must replace the final seal and secure the compromised channels." He cracked a lopsided smile that reminded her of Marcus'. "Thankfully, that's the easy part."

Sophie smiled back, then glanced behind him as the other Defenders made their way toward her.

"What now, Miracle Grow?" Olivia snarked.

Sophie crouched as the Defenders gathered around her in elemental form. "You remember our class project freshman year?" she asked Olivia.

Olivia sighed knowingly. "Let me guess. We gotta plant a tree and make it grow."

"Yep."

"Bring it on," Cedric muttered.

Sophie gathered them into a huddle. "Marcus and Olivia, make sure the ground is nice and clean. Purge any diseases or bad roots."

Marcus' jet-black silhouette and Olivia's lava form nodded in affirmation, then headed to the roots to do their work.

"Once they're done, Janet, you'll help me push the acorn close to the channels. Simon, you'll give everything a nice dousing of water like you did for me in Colorado."

Simon chuckled, and Janet saluted. "Aye aye, Persephone."

"What about me?" Cedric asked.

"You'll help me at the very end," Sophie explained. "Don't worry; it's an awesome job. Former Headmistress Case did it my freshman year here, along with my bestie Char." She winked at her best friend, who stood near the front of the expectant crowd behind them.

Charlotte winked and waved. "*You're* gonna do it this time, girl."

Sophie nodded.

Marcus and Olivia made quick work of the ground. "We burned the old leaves and mixed the ash in," Olivia noted. "Should give it some good nutrients." She high-fived Marcus, then shivered. "Geez, Prince Death. I can't even with your creepiness right now."

Marcus flashed her an apologetic smile.

Sophie nodded. "Awesome, guys. You ready, Janet?"

Janet beamed. "Ready!"

They walked toward the acorn. Sophie waited as Janet stood near the base of the trunk and twisted her arm above the earth.

A hole formed through the charred dirt, and Sophie guided the acorn down the tunnel with her life gift. Her mind crackled with wild elemental energy from the channels, loose and chaotic without Thicket Hall to keep it under control.

She got as close to it as she could, then let the acorn fall.

Janet quickly piled healthy earth over it. Simon stepped up next to her and sent a generous but gentle stream of water down the tunnel.

Janet closed the hole she'd made and knitted the ground split by Azdaja's arrival back together.

Sophie took a deep breath. "Everyone gather around and hold hands. We're going to resuscitate Thicket Hall."

Cheers and whoops erupted around her, and the entire army gathered at the base of Thicket Hall as Sophie wrapped her arms around the trunk.

"We're bringing you back, old friend," she whispered. She reached back to grasp the arm of the first person in the human chain, but many hands touched her shoulders. As she glanced back, she saw Olivia and Marcus in human form, along with the other Defenders.

"Wasn't here the first time you did this, princess," Marcus noted. There were tears in his eyes. "Show us what you're made of."

"You got this, Miracle Grow," Olivia added.

Sophie beamed, then pressed herself against the trunk of Thicket Hall, relishing the familiar scent and rough texture of its bark.

She called her life magic, which was almost overwhelming and tingled from the others' magic flowing through her. With a joyous sigh, she let it flow through the behemoth, and her psionic presence guided it to the acorn they'd buried close to the channels. In her mind's eye, she saw it turning gold-green and sprouting tiny hairy green shoots that sought Simon's water greedily.

She fed it a steady stream of life energy and saw its growth as if in a time-lapse video. The roots clutched Janet's clean and healthy soil and dipped into the chaotic channels. As soon as the baby roots touched the magic, Sophie felt a familiar rumble in her mind. Growth accelerated exponentially under the influence of both the channels' magic and her warm life gift.

Concepts formed in her mind, as they had the first time she'd spoken to Thicket Hall what felt like centuries ago. Darkness, the feeling of being small and yet immense and powerful simultaneously, warmth and the sweet smell of soil and water blending.

Then a tentative word in her mind. *Sapling?*

Sophie choked out a relieved sob and pressed her face to the trunk. *Yes! I'm here. We're all here. We're bringing you back!*

Yep, what Miracle Grow said, Olivia added with an elated laugh.

So glad to hear your voice again, Marcus added. He squeezed Sophie's shoulder.

Intense warmth washed over her. *You did it, saplings!* The roots grew longer and faster, curling over one another, joining the existing roots and filling them with new life. The chaotic buzz from the channels gradually quieted under Thicket Hall's dampening influence.

A deep sigh of awe emerged from the crowd behind her.

"It's turning brown again," someone noted.

"Look at the branches!" another cried.

Sophie glanced up to see new shoots growing from the bare boughs. She laughed and pressed the life energy through Thicket Hall faster.

Can take it from here, sapling. Energy you give good. Need a gentle touch, though, for leaves. There was a teasing quality to its voice.

Sophie caught Cedric's gaze. "You ready?"

He nodded. "Just tell me what to do, sis."

Sophie stepped away from Thicket Hall and took his hand. "We're gonna send a breeze through the branches. Like a summer wind, full of life and sunlight."

"Gotcha." Cedric called air magic, and Sophie pooled gold life energy in her hand.

Together, they lifted their free hands and sent their magic swirling into the boughs.

The soft sigh of a breeze greeted their ears, and Sophie watched with glee as leaf buds formed on the bare wood. Foliage appeared little by little, urged on by the cheers and raucous whoops of the crowd until Thicket Hall's familiar canopy had returned in full.

Cedric and Sophie lowered their arms and high-fived while the other four Defenders and their army crowded around them.

You did it, saplings! Thicket Hall exulted in their minds. *Knew you could. Unstoppable, you are.*

Sophie laughed and cried as she hugged the Defenders. She finally let go of her form and stood in their midst. She wobbled on her feet as exhaustion took hold, then pressed a hand to her stomach as it soured.

Apparently, her Defender form had kept her from feeling nausea and weakness. Now that she knew the real reason for it, that made sense.

Blissful, shocking sense.

"Careful there, Persephone," Marcus quipped. He steadied her against his chest and kissed her, one of his heart-melting, lingering kisses. "It's done, princess."

He sighed. "The battle is over."

In a contented daze, Sophie nodded.
They were finally done.

CHAPTER TWENTY-FIVE

Sophie felt she'd hugged everyone on the face of the planet by the time she got around to leading the injured to Nurse Bonnie's office. She traipsed through the mangled campus, threading through EBI agents cleaning up and passing Headmistress Rogers, who barked orders and charred debris to ash with her fire magic.

As she opened the door with Peter slung between her and Marcus, Nurse Bonnie tutted playfully.

"Why is it always you bringing a cartload of patients?" she quipped.

"Hey, at least it wasn't dodgeball this time," Sophie answered. She helped Peter onto a bed and examined his sprained ankle, then groaned as a wave of nausea threatened to knock her on her backside.

"You don't look so good," Peter told her. "Maybe you ought to go rest."

"I'm fine," Sophie retorted. "I'm not gonna let a little queasiness get me down after what we just did." She began to wrap his ankle, but Marcus grasped her hands.

"Let me do it," he insisted. "You go sit for a sec, and as soon as I'm done with Pete, we'll get you home."

"I don't *want* to go home," Sophie protested. "I want to help." She stifled a burp as Marcus nudged her out of the way and took over wrapping.

"Girl, you look greener than grass," Charlotte offered as she bustled in.

"Get her out of here, would you?" Marcus told Charlotte. "She's gonna work herself to death."

"What else is new?" Charlotte hauled Sophie up and walked out to the porch with her. She settled Sophie on a rocking chair, then sat next to her. "You done good today, girl. Trust me, the last thing anybody wants you to do is keel over."

"I know, Char. I just want to stay and help." Sophie sighed. She glanced at her churning stomach, then softened as she recalled with a thrill *why* she was so sick. It didn't make the nausea go away, but it made it easier to endure.

"Girl, why you smiling like that?" Char teased.

"I'm happy we won the battle," Sophie retorted.

Char raised an eyebrow. "I never did finish asking you that question."

Sophie's eyes went wide. She knew what Char was about to ask, and as usual, her bestie was spot on.

Char glanced around. "You said you ain't had a cycle for a while. You think it's possible you're growing something extra special in there?" She eyed Sophie's tummy.

Sophie's face reddened, and she bit her lip. She knew she wouldn't be able to keep it from her best friend, but only Marcus and the Templetons were aware of the truth. Her parents didn't even know yet.

"You are, ain't you?" Char squealed.

"Hush, Char!" Sophie clamped a hand over her friend's mouth. "No one knows yet! I didn't even know until earlier."

"For real?" Charlotte squeaked, her voice muffled by Sophie's hand. She gathered Sophie into a hug, quivering with excitement.

Sophie couldn't help but laugh. "You have to promise not to say anything, okay? I only found out because of the Serpent." She blinked in shock when the name didn't make her shiver.

"Oh, my heavens," Charlotte murmured. "That thing was the one who told you?"

Sophie nodded. "Apparently, our little plan to break the curse wasn't working because…well." She patted her tummy. "I've got the youngest Templeton safe in here."

Charlotte squealed again and squeezed Sophie. "I'm gonna be an auntie!"

"Not so tight, Char." Sophie gasped, then laughed when Char abruptly let her go. "Promise you won't tell until we've announced it to everyone."

Charlotte locked pinkies with Sophie. "You can count on me, girl."

Marcus stepped onto the porch and Charlotte went rigid, pressing her lips together in a tight line.

"You ready to go home, babe?" he asked Sophie, giving Charlotte a quizzical look.

"Yeah." Sophie chuckled. "Char, quit looking like you're constipated." She glanced at Marcus. "I told her. I couldn't hide it from her."

"Told her what?" Marcus asked. Sophie patted her

tummy, and his pale cheeks went pink. "Oh." He grinned shyly. "Right."

Charlotte let out the breath she'd been holding and squealed again. "Fool! I tell you what, I didn't expect it to happen *that* fast!"

"Char!" Sophie and Marcus clamped their hands over Charlotte's mouth as she shook with laughter. "Hush!"

"Okay, okay. I'm done! I'm sorry." Charlotte batted their hands away, then moved her fingers over her lips like a zipper. "I won't say anything, I promise."

"I'm counting on you," Sophie scolded. "Let me know how everyone is later, okay?"

"I got you, girl." Charlotte helped Sophie out of the rocking chair and led her to Marcus. "You go home. Get some sleep, and drink peppermint tea. It's great for nausea."

"Thanks, Char." Sophie hugged her best friend again. "I'm so glad I have you."

"Same, girl." Charlotte kissed her cheek, and Marcus led her away.

"Can we stop here?" Sophie pointed at the grocery store near their home. "I need to grab some peppermint tea."

"Sure." Marcus pulled in and parked close to the door. "You want me to go in for you?"

"No," Sophie protested. She laughed when Marcus arched an eyebrow. "I want to get up and walk."

"If you're sure," he relented.

Sophie smiled reassuringly, then got out and hurried

inside. She managed to find the peppermint tea without much trouble, but as she navigated to the family planning aisle, her cheeks burned. She knew Azdaja hadn't been lying, but she wanted to find out in the normal way. A test she could grasp. Something she could hold onto and see with her own eyes.

She found a two-pack of pregnancy tests and slipped them into her basket, then hurriedly went through the self-checkout and darted back to the car.

"That was quick," Marcus told her as she buckled in.

Sophie laughed. "I just want to get home. It's been a long day."

Marcus snorted. "That's putting it mildly."

They drove home in a tired, amiable silence, and Sophie went inside and headed for the bathroom after leaving the tea on the kitchen counter.

As she pulled the tests from their packaging, her hands trembled.

"What is *wrong* with me?" she whispered. "I just fought a giant dragon. This should *not* be scary."

She took a deep breath to calm her nerves, then took the test, fumbling with the instructions as she did so. When she was finished, she dropped a washcloth over the little window so she wouldn't peek at it early and washed her hands.

Marcus knocked on the door, and she jumped with a squeak.

"Sorry, princess," Marcus called. "Just wanted to say I made you tea."

"Thanks, babe," Sophie replied, cursing the tremble in her voice.

"You okay?"

Sophie took another deep breath. "Yes."

"You hesitated."

Sophie chuckled and unlocked the door.

Marcus stepped inside. He glanced at the washrag on the counter and saw the end of the test peeking out.

"Ah." He pulled her into a hug as her cheeks reddened. "Wanted to find out the scientific way, hmm?"

Sophie nodded, not trusting herself to speak.

"How long until we can look?"

"A couple of minutes," Sophie replied.

Marcus held her while they waited, and Sophie relaxed as his familiar scent surrounded her.

Finally, he let go and inched toward the test. "Now?"

Sophie laughed. "Sure. Go ahead."

He lifted the washcloth, and Sophie read the instructions to decipher what they were looking at.

"It says if it's a horizontal line, it's negative, but if it's a plus sign, it's positive," she informed him. She compared the sample image to the test, and her breath caught in her throat.

That was a plus sign. Dark, too—darker than the example on the instructions and darker than the control line.

Marcus choked, then laughed. "It's true."

"Oh, my gosh." Sophie sighed. Tears pricked her eyes, and she stared incredulously at Marcus. "We're gonna be *parents.*"

Marcus sobbed and pulled Sophie against him. She buried her face in his chest and wept tears of joy and shock. She was utterly humbled.

"Are we ready for this?" she whispered. "Can we handle it?"

Marcus gathered his wits and pushed her to arm's length, then gazed earnestly and confidently into her eyes.

"If we can face a dragon of chaos, we can handle a sweet little newborn," he encouraged.

Sophie chuckled. "Maybe you're right."

"Life hasn't stopped, Sophie," Marcus continued. "It never will, and that's a good thing. We're on to the next great adventure, the next mountain to climb together, and we're gonna rock it like always."

Sophie beamed at him.

He kissed her, and Sophie laughed when she bumped into the bathroom door.

Marcus glanced around sheepishly, then grinned at his wife. "We might need a bigger place if we're gonna be a family of three, though."

"For sure," Sophie agreed. "We'd better get house hunting then, *mon cher.*"

Marcus glanced at the positive test on the counter again, and his eyes filled with tears. Then he smiled, wrapped his arm around her waist, and led her to where her peppermint tea waited on the table.

CHAPTER TWENTY-SIX

Sophie's next week was a blur of cleanup efforts at the school, punctuated by drinking peppermint tea to stave off her nausea but with blessedly normal hours. After two months of overtime, her body needed the break. Thicket Hall's jubilant presence echoed through the Defenders' minds as they worked to repair the damage the Serpent had done to the campus. There were charred patches of grass near the edge of the forest where Marcus had tried to keep Azdaja away from Sophie, a human silhouette burned into the side of Roscoe's barn from Connor's transformation, and the pile of earth Janet had called up to keep the boys from breaking their necks.

The water building had taken the most damage, but since it had been built to withstand constant drenching, the wave of water that had crashed into it only required a good scrubbing with bleach and a few days of sitting with its windows open to clear up the mildew.

Thicket Hall had scars on its roots and gouges on the ground in front of it from the Serpent's claws, but Headmistress Rogers shooed the Defenders away when they turned to it on the last weekend before the new semester was due to start.

"That will heal in time. Besides, we're going to put a memorial here. The scars tell a story, and I want all future students who come to this school to learn from that story." Her eyes twinkled with respect as she gazed at Sophie and the others.

Later that night, the EBI hosted a gala in celebration and invited everyone who'd helped. Sophie's parents and sister were there, as were all her friends. Even Darla made an appearance with a cluster of guards.

Sadly, Gregory couldn't come, and his sentence hadn't been commuted, though the execution date had been moved out. It gave Sophie, Marcus, and the others at the EBI time to gather a legal team to appeal it. Considering Gregory's vital advice and assistance at crucial points in the battle, Sophie harbored a good deal of hope that they could save him.

Marcus found Sophie at the food table as she perused the options for something to settle her stomach. He wrapped his arms around her waist and kissed her cheek. "You ready?"

Sophie's heart flipped. They were about to announce their secret since everyone they loved and held dear was in the same room. "I think so."

Marcus took her hand and led her toward the microphone. Dottie stepped in front of it, and at a glance from Marcus, she smiled and nodded.

"Good evening, everyone!" she called into the mic. The chatter died, and they all looked at the radiant redhead expectantly. "I hope you're all enjoying this shindig in honor of our Defenders and the army that fought by their side."

Raucous cheers rose from the crowd.

"Our Life and Death Defenders have a very special message they'd like to share with you. We'd like to ask their family to move to the front if you don't mind."

Sophie worried her bottom lip with her teeth as the crowd shifted. Darla hurried to the front, holding a phone in front of her. Gregory was able to speak via FaceTime, and he smiled knowingly at Marcus and Sophie from the screen. Timothy stood next to Darla, and Sophie could tell from his tense body language that he wasn't sure what to think of Darla's and Gregory's new attitude. Still, he flashed his sister-in-law and brother a smile.

Next to Timothy stood Robert, rocking on his heels like Marcus sometimes did when he was nervous or uncomfortable. Sophie smiled comfortingly at him, and he grinned and winked at her.

The Briggses filed up next. Sophie couldn't hide a smile as Walter and Joyce waved. They didn't know yet, and she couldn't *wait* to see their reaction. She'd told Charlotte to shower them with confetti when they heard the news, and her best friend stood obediently behind them at the ready. She winked at Sophie and Marcus and gave a thumbs-up.

Sophie breathed deeply and stepped in front of the mic.

The crowd burst into applause as she adjusted its height, then laughed as she accidentally caused feedback.

"Sorry!" she squeaked, then laughed nervously.

More laughter followed. Marcus wrapped his arm around her waist and nodded when she glanced at him.

"We're really happy to see you all here tonight," Sophie began. "We couldn't have won this fight without you, that's for sure. There are so many names we could drop, and if I went down the list, I'd be here all night."

"Legit," Marcus added to the amusement of the crowd.

"However, there was a secret ingredient in our victory," Sophie went on. "Only a few of you know about it. The Serpent thought it would lead to our defeat, but instead, it all but ensured our success."

She gulped, and tears burned her eyes. "When everyone fell and I faced Azdaja alone, I didn't think I would be here tonight. She seemed intent on fulfilling the Templeton curse by taking my life, and I wasn't sure why. I forced her to tell me since I wanted to understand."

The crowd quieted. They gazed at her intently, latched onto every word.

"Then she told me something I'd never want to hear from a gigantic chaos-driven dragon," Sophie continued. "I would have much rather discovered it with my husband standing beside me, not lying unconscious at my feet and my friends hurt and unable to fight behind me."

Sophie wiped her eyes, then gazed at her parents and smiled at Millie. She exchanged knowing glances with Darla and Gregory. "She told me that I was carrying the youngest Templeton."

Startled gasps came from the crowd.

"What all that means, guys," Sophie went on, grinning at her parents' shell-shocked expressions, "is that Marcus and I are expecting, and having our little one to protect gave us the courage to keep fighting."

"Dang, son! That was *fast!*" Peter's teasing shout startled the crowd into reacting, some with laughter, some with expressions of shock.

Applause started with Dottie, who stared at them affectionately with her eyes watering. Soon the entire crowd was whooping and hollering.

Sophie laughed and raised her voice to be heard over the ruckus. She looked first at her gaping parents. "Mom, Dad, you're gonna be grandparents."

On cue, Charlotte released confetti over their heads. Walter dissolved into sobs while Joyce hugged him.

"Mr. and Mrs. Templeton, you'll be able to see your grandchild grow up without the curse," Sophie went on, waving at the Templetons. They gave her watery smiles in return.

"Robert, you're gonna be a granddad."

Robert pumped his fist. "Didn't wait, did you?" he yelled over the hubbub.

Sophie and Marcus laughed. She caught sight of her little sister dancing around her hugging parents.

"Mills, you're gonna be an aunt!" she called. "Just in time for your first year at the school."

"YES!" Millie shouted in return. "All my friends will be so jealous!"

Marcus cackled. "That's my little sis, all right," he teased. He pulled Sophie close and kissed her before they were swamped with hugs from the Briggses and the Templetons.

"I'm so thrilled for you! You'll be wonderful parents," Joyce encouraged as she hugged them both.

"You'll be a wonderful grandma, Mom," Sophie replied.

"Grandma before forty," Joyce murmured. Her eyes glistened as she laughed. "I didn't see it coming, but I'm over the moon."

"Speak for yourself," Walter grumped as he wiped his red eyes. "Now I gotta deal with a daughter who can't keep anything down."

Sophie laughed as Walter pulled her into a hug, then eyed Marcus suspiciously as he let go.

"You'd best be taking care of her, son," he scolded. "It's half your fault, you know."

Marcus' face went beet red. "Um. Yes, sir. Of course, sir."

Walter smirked, threw his arms around Marcus, and patted his back. "You know I'm just teasing."

Marcus laughed.

The Templetons stepped forward next. Timothy smiled and shook Marcus' hand, then Darla hugged Marcus.

"You will make an amazing father," Darla told him. She patted his cheek, then handed Marcus her phone and turned to Sophie. "You, darling girl, have brought light and joy to our family. It seems you are capable of nothing else." She took Sophie's hands and squeezed them. "Because of you, the curse is broken at last," Gregory added, his voice tinny through the phone though his tender smile came through clearly. "It seems life truly does triumph over death."

Sophie shook her head. "Life and death are a team." She glanced at Marcus, who studied her affectionately. "Death is the beginning of new life, and all life ends in death. They're inseparable."

Gregory's eyes twinkled as he pondered her words, then he nodded.

"Precisely, my dear."

GET SMOKED OR GO HOME

They say she's not good enough for the family business. Maybe it's because she was meant for something better.

Sometimes what looks like the worst day ever, is the beginning of our best adventure.

Idina takes that first step into a new life and gets the hell away from them to forge her own future.

But her calling is the one thing they are the most against. She joins the military just like Uncle Rick. The other family outcast.

A new Warrior is about to find out the true roots of the Moorfield name. Nothing will ever be the same.

<u>AVAILABLE ON AMAZON AND KINDLE UNLIMITED!</u>

Get sneak peeks, exclusive giveaways, behind the scenes content, and more. PLUS you'll be notified of special **one day only fan pricing** on new releases.

Sign up today to get free stories.

Visit: https://marthacarr.com/read-free-stories/

AUTHOR NOTES - MARTHA CARR

JUNE 8, 2023

Today's topic is joy. It's mostly because it keeps popping up in front of me. A friend was talking about it over dinner last night and someone else sent me a GIF with a catchy saying about joy and yet another started talking about it over a Zoom call this afternoon.

Okay, I get it, I get it.

It's also got my attention because one thing I've learned, definitions of words, particularly the ones related to emotions, are more fluid than we often realize.

Hang with me on this for a second.

There's the basic definition. A feeling of great pleasure or delight. But after that, I bring myself and my beliefs and my experiences to the table and things get a little more slippery. In my younger days, joy was a fleeting feeling that triggered doubts about what was going wrong. Yeah, that's kind of twisted, but it's where I was in life. It felt like a rollercoaster that started with a sense of ease and that some good fortune had landed on me and then rolled into doubt while I tried to bring back that initial wave of, well, joy. I also related it too much to outward events.

I thought joy was tied to what was actually happening around me. Do you see what I mean?

For me, joy was channeled through fear and influenced my life differently than, say, someone who experiences joy more simply. Like as a choice.

That's where I've come to these days. Joy is now a choice about how I feel about what's going on around me, and can be mine at any time, in varying amounts, and is largely fueled by gratitude. For me, it's no longer so mercurial and fleeting. I changed, the definition changed and expanded. Bonus for me, I stopped thinking others could 'take my joy' or that I needed to be around people who agreed with me on a list of topics in order to feel joy.

Now, my definition says, it's not tied to others at all. It's within me and can be called upon at any moment.

Here's part two of the whole joy thing and why I'm paying attention to the fact that the universe keeps showing it to me right now. My awareness that joy is created by me based on where I'm putting my attention, is changing where I'm putting my attention. Because that has changed, my perspective on how things operate in general in life has changed. That is one of the most powerful things that can happen to a body and why people will pay a lot of money for therapy.

It's also why we will obstinately argue a point even when it's not in our best interests – because our belief system says, 'this is a truth' and we forgot, no, it was just an idea somewhere in the beginning. Change the perspective, we can change our mind.

So, back to joy. Now that I grasp it as a choice regardless of where I am or who I'm with, and fueled by gratitude, (helped along by forgiveness, by the way), I can use that in moments of fear or doubt to keep going. Fear still finds me, just not in such large amounts, and now I have these tools to help me sort it out and feel joy again. Gratitude being the first tool. That has helped me create a bigger life, do more in my career that I want to be doing and try things without knowing the outcome – and feel joy on the journey instead of waiting for the end result. More adventures to follow.

AUTHOR NOTES - MICHAEL ANDERLE

JUNE 5, 2023

First, thank you for not only reading this story but these author notes in the back as well!

GARY! GARY!

Every author is shaped by the influences they encountered early in life, and for me, a major influence was E. Gary Gygax.

If the name rings a bell, it's because Gygax was one of the co-creators of the role-playing game Dungeons & Dragons.

I was a teenager in the eighties, captivated by the fantastic worlds Gygax had created and the dungeon modules I could read that allowed my imagination freedom.

The descriptions in his stories painted vivid landscapes where mythical creatures roamed and epic adventures unfolded and dark elves stabbed your ass.

This wasn't just a game. It was a full immersion into a universe where anything could happen, and ordinary people could become heroes.

When I moved into writing a few decades later, Gygax's influence stayed with me, particularly in the urban fantasy genre.

The beauty of urban fantasy lies in the juxtaposition of the familiar and the extraordinary. As Gygax did with D&D, I strive to craft intricate worlds that are tangible yet mysterious, grounded yet unbounded. I want my readers to feel like they've stepped into another world, yet one that's nestled within their own, just around the corner or through a hidden door.

While I've grown and evolved as a writer, the echoes of those early days, engrossed in a D&D campaign and his books, reverberate through my work. They remind me of why I fell in love with fantasy.

I can only hope to recreate that feeling of awe and excitement in the stories I help create.

Have a great week or weekend, and I look forward to chatting with you in the next book!

Ad Aeternitatem,

Michael Anderle

MORE STORIES with Michael newsletter HERE: https://michael.beehiiv.com/

BOOKS BY MARTHA CARR

THE LEIRA CHRONICLES
CASE FILES OF AN URBAN WITCH
DIARY OF A DARK MONSTER
THE EVERMORES CHRONICLES
SOUL STONE MAGE
THE KACY CHRONICLES
MIDWEST MAGIC CHRONICLES
THE FAIRHAVEN CHRONICLES
I FEAR NO EVIL
THE DANIEL CODEX SERIES
SCHOOL OF NECESSARY MAGIC
SCHOOL OF NECESSARY MAGIC: RAINE CAMPBELL
ALISON BROWNSTONE
FEDERAL AGENTS OF MAGIC
SCIONS OF MAGIC
THE UNBELIEVABLE MR. BROWNSTONE
DWARF BOUNTY HUNTER
ACADEMY OF NECESSARY MAGIC
MAGIC CITY CHRONICLES
ROGUE AGENTS OF MAGIC
CHRONICLES OF WINLAND UNDERWOOD
WITCH WARRIOR

OTHER BOOKS BY JUDITH BERENS

OTHER BOOKS BY MARTHA CARR

JOIN THE ORICERAN UNIVERSE FAN GROUP ON FACEBOOK!

BOOKS BY MICHAEL ANDERLE

Sign up for the LMBPN email list to be notified of new releases and special deals!

http://lmbpn.com/email/

For a complete list of books by Michael Anderle, please visit:

www.lmbpn.com/ma-books/

CONNECT WITH THE AUTHORS

Martha Carr Social
Website:
http://www.marthacarr.com
Facebook:
https://www.facebook.com/groups/MarthaCarrFans/

Michael Anderle

Website: http://lmbpn.com

Email List: https://michael.beehiiv.com/

https://www.facebook.com/LMBPNPublishing

https://twitter.com/MichaelAnderle

https://www.instagram.com/lmbpn_publishing/

https://www.bookbub.com/authors/michael-anderle

www.ingramcontent.com/pod-product-compliance
Lightning Source LLC
LaVergne TN
LVHW041800060526
838201LV00046B/1065